Here Kitty Kitty

"A Tribeca restaurant manager, Lee makes a late-morning Scotch, after snorting coke all night, seem whimsically glamorous.... There are no easy epiphanies in this dark, tender book. Libaire instead wisely explores her heroine's long and difficult struggle to take care of herself: to be sober, to sleep peacefully, to be alone. In the process, the author offers glittering descriptions of New York life, both its obstacles and its promise."

—Suzy Hansen, *New York Times Book Review*

"Darkly comic ... cribbed from the breathless pages of *Interview* and *New York* magazines."

—*Los Angeles Times*

"*Here Kitty Kitty* brings the streets of New York alive with beautiful poetic prose, and like a bottle of expensive champagne, it tastes of bittersweet sadness once it's gone. Like John O'Hara's *BUtterfield 8*, *Here Kitty Kitty* shows a woman struggling from the bottom and sinking even deeper, making roadkill of the men who fall under her spell, while searching for something more meaningful than money, or even love."

—Michael Hornburg, author of *Bongwater* and *Downers Grove*

"*Author reminds me of:* Truman Capote and Jack Kerouac, when both were at the top of their game. Lee also would get along fine with the ever-willful Ivich from Sartre's war trilogy. *Best reason to read:* This is a marvelous book! This stream-of-consciousness novel does a superb job of depicting a self-destructive artist, and the city itself."

—Ed Halloran, *Rocky Mountain News*

"The fine line between distraction and madness is one that Jardine Libaire's narrator, Lee, crosses several times. This novel draws a remarkable picture of the romance of self-destruction—all the attractions of what is bad for you—and, also, of the more difficult 'pyrotechnics of faith.'"

—Charles Baxter, author of *Saul and Patsy* and
The Feast of Love

"Libaire may be ahead of her game."

—Pauline M. Millard, *Associated Press*

"As one might expect from the come-hither title, the protagonist of *Here Kitty Kitty* walks that tightrope between sophisticate and psycho."

—DailyCandy.com, "Cracking the Books: Bad Girls"

"Libaire is talented, no question."

—Alynda Wheat, *Entertainment Weekly*

"Libaire's voice is urgent, tough, and elegant. She takes a classic story—of a young woman unraveling at the seams—and gives it the poetry of a fairy tale. Lee is a haunting urban archetype. She swills pink champagne for breakfast, snorts coke on the job, and, with a cheerful nihilism, veers closer and closer to prostitution. *Here Kitty Kitty* documents the secret rites of passage into a certain variety of American womanhood. It reflects the excitement, sadness, and trashy glamour of New York."

—Lisa Dierbeck, author of *One Pill Makes You Smaller*

"Libaire jams her paragraphs with fractured images of the cityscape, brand-name clothing, trendy neighborhoods, and after-hours clubs. . . . Quite a few readers will be seduced by her cinematic writing and her vulnerable hipsters."

—Joanne Wilkinson, *Booklist*

"*Here Kitty Kitty*'s heroine, Lee, reads like an old friend. Hard, soft, funny, and dangerously out of control but relentlessly lovable. An affectionate and completely believable slice of New York's not-so-young and reckless, distinctive for its unapologetic tone and finely observed details."

—Anthony Bourdain, author of *Kitchen Confidential* and
A Cook's Tour

"With *Here Kitty Kitty*, Jardine Libaire gives chick lit a swift kick in the rump. She writes with a clipped, cinematic panache, and her deadpan decadence will remind readers of an East Coast version of Joan Didion's *Play It As It Lays* and Bret Easton Ellis's *Less Than Zero*."

—Kurt Wenzel, author of *Gotham Tragic* and *Lit Life*

"They say the best nonfiction reads like fiction. But is the reverse also true? It would seem so after reading this gorgeously written debut novel, whose narrator is so keenly evoked that her reminiscences read like a memoir. . . . Laced with musings about art and marked by unexpected metaphors, the book summons consistently powerful images. . . . Those looking for a darker, more literary slant of chick lit would do well to check this out. Libaire's fashion sense is as well honed as her perfectly turned phrases."

—*Publishers Weekly*

"*Here Kitty Kitty* is a first novel possessed of an impressive grace and restraint, which provides a sharp contrast to the reckless existence of its heroine. Living dangerously can be a tiresome subject, but nothing about this novel is predictable, including how engaged readers will become with Lee's struggle to interrupt her own descent. Jardine Libaire is a delightful writer and I look forward to being surprised by her next novel."

—Katharine Weber, author of *The Music Lesson* and
The Little Women

Here Kitty Kitty

A NOVEL

Jardine Libaire

HOGARTH

NEW YORK / LONDON

Copyright © 2004 by Jardine Raven Libaire
Excerpt from *White Fur* copyright © 2017 by Jardine Raven Libaire

All rights reserved.
Published in the United States by Hogarth, an imprint of
the Crown Publishing Group,
a division of Penguin Random House LLC, New York.
crownpublishing.com

HOGARTH is a trademark of the Random House Group Limited,
and the H colophon is a trademark of Penguin Random House LLC.

Originally published in hardcover in the United States by
Little, Brown and Company, New York, in 2004.
Subsequently published in paperback in the United States by
Back Bay Books, New York, in 2005.

Library of Congress Cataloging-in-Publication Data is available upon request.

ISBN 978-0-525-57449-1
Ebook ISBN 978-0-525-57450-7

PRINTED IN THE UNITED STATES OF AMERICA

Book design: Andrea Lau
Cover design: Catherine Casalino
Cover photographs: © Fabrizia Milla/Trevillion Images

10 9 8 7 6 5 4 3 2 1

First Hogarth Edition

This book is for my mother and father.

Here Kitty Kitty

ONE

⟡⟡⟡⟡

The opium-eater loses none of his moral sensibilities or aspirations. He wishes and longs as earnestly as ever to realize what he believes possible, and feels to be exacted by duty; but his intellectual apprehension of what is possible infinitely outruns his power, not of execution only, but even of power to attempt.

—THOMAS DE QUINCEY,
from *Confessions of an English Opium-Eater*

One should consume Baileys in a crystal tumbler while watching Spice Hot. At jazz clubs, red wine and queen-sized, white-filtered Nat Shermans. At Hamptons polo games, a Pimm's Cup for style and a line off the dash of a police-auctioned Ferrari for effect. Crème de menthe before going down on someone who deserves it. Super Bowl Sunday, Bud cans (shotgunned) and Ritalin (crushed and snorted). A boxing match on a hotel room TV, Maker's Mark Manhattans (up, three cherries) and petite ham sandwiches on a silver tray. White Castle and Remy Red for a dogfight. While wrapping Christmas presents, Pabst Blue Ribbon and pizza. For suicidal depression on a weekday morning, pink champagne. Before a job interview, Irish coffee and Xanax. Straight tequila on your birthday. And on that night that rolls out of the blue unknown future into the lap of the present, when a lady realizes the game is over, that kind of evening calls for martinis: stock gin, filthy, up, no olives.

I found this list scrawled on a series of cocktail napkins, stuffed into a gold clutch. Belinda and I must have written it one night a couple years ago. This was our religion. Actually, it was more important; it was art. But one day, the things that make you free start to keep you down.

The beginning of the end began with a vision.

I'd twisted all night to Brazilian records at Black Betty. A strawberry-blond cornrowed kid in a Lakers jersey cut lines for me in the men's room. At home, I drank warm milk with brandy. I leaned back in my orange butterfly chair and calculated the money I owed. It was uncountable.

Outside, the night sky turned turquoise at the horizon, highlighting a clutter of buildings close by, while the World Trade Towers glittered in the distance, across Brooklyn, on the other side of the East River. I fell asleep sometime before the sun came up.

I dreamed I was lying in a bathtub full of oatmeal, like the soak my mother made when I had chicken pox. Around my neck, dropping to my sternum like a necklace, lay a ring of blisters. I understood them in the dream to be "fever pearls." From above, I looked down on my body, on my bloated white form, and knew the pulsing marks to be pockets of toxins locked under my skin.

I woke to sunlight, clutching a teddy bear that hadn't existed in many years.

I'd waited half an hour and was late for work. Anthony leaned against his Escalade, beefy arms crossed, talking to someone hidden under the keyboard awning. I owed him three months of rent, and soon, September. I bit my nails and watched through my cheap lace curtain.

I paced. Checked the time on my phone every thirty seconds. Opened the fridge once more: a few Rheingolds and a pink gel eye mask. Eggs and orange juice hadn't materialized. Stopped in front of the mirror to curse my baby face again. The dimple in my chin, the pucker under my eyes that made me look sleepy even when I was wired, my pout, my long, dark-red hair and Bettie Page bangs: these features conspired against me. I looked exactly like a girl who wouldn't pay rent.

Finally he left, and I ran down the stairs.

Everyone still wore leather, even though it was a hundred degrees, squinting as they emerged from steamy buildings with bulldogs. Cars cruised, windows open, bass thumping. Girls walked to summer school pushing strollers. Boys strutted down the sidewalk, earphones around necks, diamonds in both ears. A hydrant exploded, crystal in the haze.

Air conditioners leaked down from windows. Plastic bags floated across empty basketball courts. A fat white kid, shirt hung around neck like scarf, walked in the middle of the street with an ice cream melting off the cone faster than he could lick it.

"Lee."

Anthony was sitting at an outdoor table. We fought in low, restrained voices. Then he offered me two weeks to pay up. Otherwise, he warned, eviction.

"I'll do it legal, Lee, but I'll put your stuff on the street. You know I will."

"You're some friend," I said.

He laughed, looked at the sky, shaking his head. "I'm not your friend."

Old Polish ladies sat on stoops and appraised me. I straightened my shoulders, sauntered past them without smiling.

I was at least fifty-five K in the hole. Spread around on credit cards, personal loans (i.e., friends who wouldn't return my calls anymore), back taxes, medical and utility bills.

I was a wild card at spending money. I shopped like a Dadaist. When Belinda found out she had herpes, I sent eight dozen white roses to her apartment. Sometimes, if I felt low, I copied Warhol and bought myself a birthday cake. One Saturday night, Sherry and I rented a white limousine to drive us through the city, over bridges, through tunnels, and eventually to a McDonald's drive-through in Brooklyn.

A couple years ago, Belinda and I met for lunch, which turned into afternoon martinis. It accelerated, and then we were in the back of a Town Car choosing pills from the bento box of drugs in the console.

Next I remember snow and making some sort of scene at Bergdorf's.

I'd woken up the following morning with that feeling I wasn't alone. Like when you open your eyes, and without turning around, without hearing breathing, without feeling warmth, you know there's a man in your bed. Dragged myself from the sheets and tripped into the kitchen. On the floor, a half-eaten piece of Wonder bread and a hot-pink cocktail umbrella. And there it was, lying across the table.

A white knee-length fur. Square black buttons with the Fendi logo. Gold and black *F*s on the silk lining. *Pleased to meet you*, I thought.

Belinda used to be my partner in crime. My fellow outsider. I'd known the girl since she was a ninety-pound catalog model cracked out at System, her Australian accent rugged, her language X-rated. We used to sunbathe topless on her East Village roof, wearing white jeans and rainbow-mirrored sunglasses we'd bought on the street. After long nights, we parted ways at eight in the morning, stepping gingerly through ice in stilettos, lipstick smeared from making out with strangers in the red-lighted downstairs of clubs.

We used to stumble down Avenue A, sipping tallboys in paper bags, with no destination. I picked her up from the hospital after she fainted at a rave. She picked me up after a girl clubbed my head with a cell phone on the F train.

She could have had anyone back then. Monstrous cheekbones. Blond bob. Wicked eyes, the whites as hard as china, lashes curled back to the lid. A wide frame she used to starve to stay in business. Legs that lasted for miles. Her voice was so raspy, she'd ask for butter to be passed and men would feel she'd promised them something. She made both good and very bad choices. She'd call me from anonymous apartments. The guy's pimpled back, the dusty mirror, and no condom wrapper in sight.

Eventually I did notice a shadow, a dark thing that was chased around her face. Like a black moth behind a curtain, trying to find the way out.

A year and a half ago, she got pregnant. She freaked out, decided on abortion, but all she could do was cry in her bedroom. Matt coaxed her from the edge the way a parent beckons a toddler off thin ice in the middle of the lake — you can't go get him, you cannot frighten him, and the only way you'll save his life is to act contrary to how you feel.

Brunch shift. The Tribeca restaurant I'd managed for years, a chic converted diner, slanted like the original establishment. Mirrors framed in mother-of-pearl chips covered walls. The mosaic floor was primitive, its pieces beige, white, turquoise. The stools, whose gold sparkles reminded me of banana seats on bicycles, were pulled to a white Formica counter decorated with gold spirals and stars. We'd been written up again in *Time Out*, so all of uptown was downtown today.

The woman sent back her soup. I apologized and explained that it was meant to be rich. She was the kind of woman who made me feel like an orphan. Her highlights had been painted strand by strand, and she wore a white Marc Jacobs sundress and an aquamarine cube on her finger.

When she beckoned for the second time, I pretended not to notice.

"Miss," she said firmly. "Hello?"

"How can I help you?"

"This white you recommended, I'm afraid it's turned." Her lips pursed as though she could barely restrain a smile.

"Do you want me to taste it?" I offered.

"Um, not necessary. I mean, be my guest, if you really want to. But I know wine."

I held up one finger to indicate I'd return and walked to the bar for a new bottle. I dallied for a moment, fussing with nothing, to slow my heart rate. Then I marched back to her table and uncorked it.

"You're a doll," she said, taking a sip and winking.

Walking away, I wiped sweat from my upper lip. I'd experienced much worse than this, every day, but here I was: trembling, hot. I suddenly knew I would quit.

Yves opened the office door and looked me over with ice-gray eyes. I'd been pounding a snifter of B&B and crying. He had a way of smiling without saying anything that made me feel like a child.

Not missing a beat, he said he'd just stopped by to see me. The bartender had told him I was down here.

"I'm quitting," I said, my voice yolky. "I'm telling Brendan tonight. I'm going to call him at home."

With slender, suntanned hands, he struck a match and held it to two Dunhills. After shaking out the fire, he gave one to me.

"Quitting," I repeated. He'd seen me fall apart a hundred times, but a new note of desperation in my voice surprised us both.

He squinted at me through the smoke he'd exhaled. His eyes moved from my right eye to my left. His cuffs, undone, exposed handsome wrists.

His face was icy, Nordic, even though that wasn't his heritage. Arched eyebrows and pointed eyeteeth, plus a slant of skin over cold blue cat eyes, made for a beautiful and frightening face. His chin wasn't too small, or too delicate, but there was a fineness to its sculpted shape that lent the head a feminine dimension.

Yves was old enough to be my father. In some ways—table manners, yellow-white hair like the inside of banana skin—he seemed older, and in other ways—lithe golden body, nightlife stamina—younger.

He wore high-waisted slacks like Fred Astaire. Walked like a gentleman, as if he could break out tap-dancing. His voice rumbled in his Adam's apple: a jaguar purring, licking blood from its own teeth.

"Do you know what that bitch said to me?" I asked, and then put my hand on the phone. "I'm calling Brendan now."

"I have an idea," he said in that European murmur.

I looked at him scornfully. "What."

"Take tonight to think about it and then call him tomorrow."

This flooded my eyes again, but the tears lodged in lashes like beads. He stepped toward me, brushed one hand through my hair. He held my hand so I could go nowhere, and ordered me home.

Walking from the subway to my building, the sun beat so hard on my face I could hear my eternal sinus infection bubbling.

I dropped out of college after my freshman year and moved to Cape Cod. Two years of living like a bum there, I moved to the city, and within a couple years, I was living with Kai.

We both worked in kitchens, but he was in culinary school at the same time. Kai always pretended to be destitute, disappearing to the men's room when the check came. We were kids together. We joked about farting and fought over drugs.

Kai had a dirty mouth. He looked, with his blond crew cut and pink cheeks, like somebody's baby brother. He left two and a half years ago to apprentice in Paris. He left with no warning. I would have gone with him, even though he was an idiot.

When Kai and I made love, if it was good, I went to a dark place. Not as in morbid or sinister. Literally: a void. Occasionally, images bubbled up like gardenias surfacing, with clean petals, in a pit of tar.

I'd been seeing Yves for almost a year now. He was a regular at the restaurant, and he'd courted me politely. One day, after we'd flirted a couple months, he started sending gifts.

White-truffle oil. A black Celine scarf. Red lipstick in a gold case. This guy was bringing me Richart chocolates when I couldn't afford toilet paper. Sherry was over the morning of the first snowfall when an antique blond fur collar arrived. She tried it on, and the yellow tufts against her ebony skin looked elegant and crazy.

"You should take it," I said.

"Come on, girl. Don't give away a man's gift. You got no manners."

"It's beautiful on you."

"Maybe one day I'll borrow it," she drawled, smoking, stretching out on my couch. "It's very movie star. It's very gangster's girl."

"Fully," I agreed, turning the collar in my hands.

Each time Yves gave me something, I got sweet. It was so linear. I was a kitty cat lapping milk, swishing its tail. Because I'd been hung out to dry by Kai, these luxuries made me safe.

Yves took care of me. When I was disorderly, he looked

around the room, wide-eyed, and declared: *My God, she's a hellcat.* Or he'd get me another drink and tell me to sit down and shut up. I often got hiccups; he'd summon a lemon slice doused in bitters from the waiter, hold it to my mouth.

My only complaint was his music. At Virgin I took him through the aisles, filling his shopping basket. I slipped his old CDs to the housekeeper: Paula Abdul, Big Audio Dynamite, Hanson. I think it was a European thing. Movies, too. He watched *Titanic* eighty times. He chain-smoked as the ship went down, clutching the leather arm of the couch as though the loft were sinking too.

I eventually learned through gossip about the women right before me. The Hungarian countess sounded like a melancholic delicacy. Once in a while, she still came to Raoul's to drink wine at the bar with older men. She never spoke, never laughed. The hollows around her eyes were darkly glamorous, her mouth sullen: she had the beauty of an insomniac. I didn't know her name but called her Ophelia in my mind.

Marcelle was French like Yves, a couple years older than him, taller, and at least as tough. She'd modeled her way from a farm town to New York City at the age of sixteen. Married a series of international visionaries, amicably divorced them. Became indispensable to a couturier, and was now exalted and consulted by everyone. I saw her at a museum party. She was turned away from me: her architecture was brutal as that of an Egon Schiele subject. Black jersey clung to her and pooled on the floor. Jade chandelier earrings hung to her shoulders like rain. People said she and Yves were more expatriate siblings than lovers.

Friends had often paid me this backhanded compliment: *You're one of those girls, Lee, that needs an older man, someone who can appreciate you, a connoisseur.* But I finally understood when I got to know Yves. He was beguiled instead of bewildered by my desperate morning champagne, my fur jackets and cowboy hats, my need one day to track down Djuna Barnes's *Ladies Almanack*. He even called rare book dealers. When I decided we had to have quince jam for breakfast, or hard-boiled quail eggs for lunch, he escorted me on the hunt.

One night, we were drinking espressos after a long dinner at his loft with Guillaume, a proper, elderly Belgian. In Yves's bedroom, I changed into a white feather dress I'd bought that day at the flea market. Turned the lights down in the main room, cranked up Cypress Hill's "Tres Equis," and danced like a cabaret star. I shimmied and high-kicked. My hip knocked an end table, setting a Chinese lamp rocking on its base. Yves's eyes warned me to be careful. A feather seesawed to the floor. When I picked it up and tickled under Guillaume's chin, the old man glared, gripped the tiny bone-china handle of his cup. I put on Prince's "Delirious," but Yves got up and turned it down.

"I think that's enough, Lee. This is a shortcut to a migraine."

But here's the thing. Later in bed, I traced Yves's mouth as he smiled at the dark ceiling.

"What is it?" I whispered.

He was silent, grinning. Finally he answered. "Did you see his face? He almost tore the cup in half. I wish I'd had a camera."

Yves secretly loved chaos.

I got dressed: white capris, leopard sling backs, a dirty black mesh shirt. Bells from two churches were competing. The horizon from my window was cluttered with white-hot buildings, a turquoise mosque, smokestacks. Pigeons reeled around the sky.

I don't know how I made it to Raoul's that night, or anywhere. Every morning, I smeared on makeup, smoked a cigarette, and drank a cup of instant coffee. Sprayed perfume between legs, Binaca in mouth.

You know when your life is not adding up to more than the sum of its parts? At this point, the sum wasn't even equal to the parts; it was less. Someone was skimming.

Days off were rare, but worse than working days. I'd pace or stand by the door—could I bear to put on shoes and run errands? If not, could I bear to stay in the apartment without cigarettes? It was a draw, for hours sometimes, standing there, barefoot, paralyzed.

Way back in the day, I'd been a good-time girl. I'd made choices without thinking. I'd been a red-blooded American who dug steak, Budweiser, good sex scenes in bad movies.

On the Cape, I chambermaided at a motor lodge, lifting a pair of cuff links here, a pint of Southern Comfort there. I lived with random people, survived on clam chowder they brought home from where they worked and on hot dogs from gas stations. I smoked PCP-laced weed that made me think the trees were full of bats, not bikinis hung out to dry; learned how to race a motorcycle; fucked two guys at once; had a waterskiing accident; and eventually came back to this city bruised, uninnocent, and never prouder.

That's when I'd been strong. That's when I could drop more acid than the boys. That's when I could stay up all night, doing blow and slamming Jack Daniel's, and work all day, and do it again. I was an ox. Kai's departure was partly to blame for my disintegration. And what happened to my mother. I didn't know the exact trajectory of my breakdown, but I did know that I'd become weak, holding onto wildness, cherishing the idea of it the way you blow a dying fire.

To meet Yves, I took the L to Sixth Avenue, the 9 to Houston. My face ghostly in the violet window of the train, fragrance blooming out of my hot skin. No matter how shitty I looked, people stared: I had the smell of a fruit about to split. My flesh somehow demonstrated lethargy, as if I wanted to be lying down at all times. I was five ten, but not exactly heavy. It was the nature of my anatomy that was rich, composed as it was of foie gras, cocaine, red Zinfandel, chocolate, quaaludes, brandy.

Above ground, the night had brought nothing but darker heat. Tangerine lances shot through crevices between SoHo buildings as the sun rolled down the other side of the world. I thought to myself that something had to give. Without asking for help or admitting the scale of it, I had to talk to Yves tonight about the Armageddon of my life.

At the mouth of Raoul's, I inhaled decades of garlic clove, smoke, perfume, lamb. Yves's back was to me, his arm resting across the black leather banquette, cuff undone. Across from him, a woman's face, pale as a refrigerated gardenia, looked up sharply.

"You know Delphine, love," Yves insisted.

"I don't think I do, baby." Even though I did.

"How's your sculpture series, dear?" Delphine said. "Have you finished?"

I turned to look at her. Art was more private than sex or love—not the work itself, but the endeavor. I hated being asked, especially since I hadn't done anything in so long. So I made things up. Delphine was ceramic, like all of Yves's older women friends. If there was more than one of them, they spoke other languages when I was around. They wore Chanel suits. Front teeth yellowed by tobacco. In the afternoon, they sipped bellinis at Cipriani on West Broadway, smoked Gauloises. They weren't bad people, but I enjoyed lying to them.

"Mnh," I said pensively. "Actually I got sidetracked by a story-book I'm illustrating."

"How exciting," she said. "And how's that turning out?"

"Just great," I said evenly. "I'm almost finished."

"But you haven't even started," Yves said, smiling.

I punched him in the arm.

Delphine politely made a befuddled face.

"Martini, straight up, filthy, no olives," I begged the waiter.

She said, "Everyone these days seems to be doing a book."

I said, "That's true, Delphine. Everyone seems to be doing a book."

"May I ask what it's about?"

"Fucking, drinking, smoking, loving, living, freebasing, spending, laughing, crying, working, falling apart, kissing, writing, blacking out."

"I see."

Yves laughed. "I really can't wait to see it, Lee. I gather you're still in the research stage."

I sipped martini three and stared at my steak. Delphine had found a way to escape us. Yves watched my face. I stuck out my tongue at him.

"Is there something wrong, lamb?" he asked tightly.

"Lamb? Yves, I'm not your niece. I'm your girlfriend."

"Is there a reason you felt the need to speak that way to her?"

"I'm sure she's seen and heard worse than me."

"She's an old friend, you know."

"She's worn out."

"I'm tired of this," he said, and pressed his mouth with his napkin, folded it, and tucked it under his plate.

"You used to think it was cute," I whined.

"No, I used to tolerate it because there were other elements of you that were cute."

I sat at the table alone. Sipping another martini, I watched him smoke at the bar. What a bad start.

Yves stood, one hand in his pocket, talking to a man in a beige V-neck who flicked open and closed a gold lighter. Yves's barbered head nodded at whatever the man was saying, and he didn't look my way once. The ball was in my court. If we were to have any conversation, I had to approach him.

When I was very drunk, the world became a slide show. Sneaking up toward Yves, I looked sideways and saw a purple flame in a dark booth, light blossoming on a man's face as he drew close to the match. An anemic blonde staking a cigarette into a wedge of black cake. My own red toenail peeking from the opening of my leopard sling back.

"Hey, daddy, I need a drink." This was my way of apologizing. He looked left then right. "No one stopping you."

"Okay," I said slowly, glancing at the V-neck guy, then at Yves, trying to communicate with my eyes.

"Is there something wrong?" he asked me.

"Well, yeah," I said. "I kind of don't have any money."

He took a twenty from his wallet. "Bring me the change," he said calmly, and turned back to his friend. "As you were saying."

I walked toward the bar, but then circled back out of his line of vision. I walked to the table. Isn't it crazy how anger sometimes feels like joy? Just a crash of blood through your heart. I took his car keys from the sport coat he'd left in the booth.

The L.I.E. swarmed with kids heading from Float in the city to Conscience Point at the beach, or straight into a chintz-wallpapered bedroom at a rented mansion. A Range Rover swerved, going ninety, glow sticks floating in the backseat. Made me feel better about my own steering.

I stopped at a gas station for candy. I must have been weaving, but a cop car passed, paint shining like a shark, and never came near me. I did get the finger, for changing lanes without signaling, from a porn-star blonde in a yellow Porsche.

I drove the Lexus through Southampton, red lights blinking instead of changing. The landscape dreamy, moonlit fields of zinnias, fruit stands closed up as though they'd never offered bins of raspberries, baskets of lettuce. Everything was beautiful and frightening, deserted for the night but coming off as forever deserted.

"Bring me the change!" I'd say every once in a while in disbelief.

Ours was originally a guesthouse for the main house on the hill. The area was wooded, and my headlights severed trunks as I turned into the drive. Pulled up to the front path, cut the lights and engine, and stared until details burned out of the dark.

My mother always read on a wicker chaise under the rose tree in this yard. Bees would devour the blossoms, climbing from turquoise leaf to leaf, their bodies vibrating in the sunlight. They'd step from a petal to her knee, her skin creamy as the rose: they never knew the difference. She never flinched.

Two years ago, almost, she died in this house. I held her hand. A male hospice nurse pretended to do a jigsaw puzzle of the Manhattan skyline at our kitchen table so we had privacy.

When she was young, she'd undergone a radical mastectomy and radiation. Somehow, the underdeveloped technology had burned both lungs. The damage wasn't discovered until, at the age of fifty-nine, she suffered trouble breathing. X-rays revealed membranes around each lung. The doctor compared them to cauls, those sacs found sometimes around fetuses.

"Those are supposed to be good luck, those ones around the baby's head," I said to him.

"They are," he admitted.

"But my mother's aren't good luck."

He shook his head, looking at his shoes. "No, no they're not."

Sitting there in Yves's car, I was sure I'd mourned; I'd been grieving for almost two years, but nothing had changed. I still didn't want to go in there. Months ago, I'd come to box the remaining belongings so I could rent out the house. My mother had been an elegant woman in her own carrottop way, and it was excruciating to go through panties with elastics broken, stockings dotted with nail polish, widowed gloves stowed away just in case. Within an hour, everything I came across—the apricot slip hanging from the bedpost, a lipstick in the medicine cabinet, an abalone shell still dusty with ash—loomed and shivered like an object from a nightmare. I'd fled with the job half finished and hadn't returned until tonight.

My mother had made my childhood into a paradise. She didn't believe in ordinary life. Every day should be a kingdom, the proportions of each hour majestic, regal.

When I'd come down for breakfast in the morning, dragging my book bag on the stairs, yawning, the first thing I'd hear was my mother singing. By my plate of sugared toast: a blue jay feather. In the windows hung glass prisms, and rainbows shot their colors against the walls. To this day, when I open her books, brown wafers of red roses fall from the pages.

With pajamas on my bath-damp body, I'd find a snowbell on my pillow. My mother always told a bedtime story. Then I'd ask her to tell another, and she would. Then she'd ask me to tell one, and she'd lay on my bed with her eyes closed.

We played with lipstick. We roller-skated on a summer midnight. We ate pancakes for dinner. Once, I remember, a snow day was predicted. We woke up, and the roads were clear. But she let me stay home. We sat by the fire that whole day, the soles of our feet pinked by the flames, and strung shells onto necklaces. In the evenings, I did homework at the dinner table while she played records: June Christy, Lee Wiley, Billie Holiday. With a cigarette in one hand and a mug in the other, she danced. Red sun burned through her kimono. The fabric seemed to dissolve in the violent light. Sometimes I watched her. Sometimes I danced with her. We never turned on the lamps until we couldn't see.

But with the god gone, the house was just a house, and I couldn't bear to enter it. I adjusted the leather car seat, and closed my drunken eyes.

I rang the main house doorbell in the morning. Rolled my head on my neck to loosen kinks. Geraniums in cracked pots flanked the door. I rang again.

When I was young, I'd scrutinized Art and Rebecca. As a teenager, I'd watched their Gramercy Park apartment when they were away. I'd worn her chinchilla. Smoked resin out of his hash pipe. I'd toddled around in her sharkskin pumps, studied his dog-eared *Kama Sutra*. They were my other parents.

But after showing glimmers of artistic promise throughout school, I'd dropped out of college, run away to Harwich Port to hide out with deadheads, waitresses, methheads. They'd never said so, but I imagined Art and Becca had given up on me. They didn't have kids, and over the years they'd bought me paints, brushes, linen. They paid for a summer art session at Yale when I was sixteen. It was possible they resented my failure. If so, they concealed it, making me feel worse.

I heard slippers scuffing.

"My precious," she purred.

White caftan, black eyes. Bony hands weighted with turquoise, gold, opal, diamond. Short brown hair tucked behind ears. She set her coffee on the foyer table. The house had broken-down glamour: sand in rugs, dead dragonflies in candy bowls, drapes stained from rain.

"Where did you come from, you baby-boo?" she said.

I said it had been a long time, my mouth muffled as she hugged me.

"Lee," she rasped, floating into the courtyard. "You are *stunning*, but you look like you slept in a jail cell or something."

Art, though he'd already squeezed me to his huge chest, pinched my cheeks, and tried to force money on me, was back to reading his paper.

"Doesn't she look stunning," Becca prompted. "A little washed out, maybe."

We ate lunch. Wasps droned over melon soup, dragging stingers. Art alternated between pushing up glasses, breaking off cornbread, and passionately refolding the Sports section.

I didn't know how to bring it up, so I let her talk. Becca wandered from Janice's Vero Beach wedding to bars in Spain to Coney Island in the old days. Each time she mentioned one of her teenaged loves, she stole a glance at Art, but he wasn't biting today. Blue beams refracted through the swimming pool and crisscrossed the yard, wavering, and we smoked Becca's slim cigarettes, ashing on our cake plates.

"I'm putting the house up for sale," I finally said.

Art had always liked to sit on his patio with watercolors and easel. Painted poppies: slashes of scarlet, black beads. Jazz station on transistor radio. I once found him watering impatiens naked.

But he was lawyer to mobsters, boxers, Wall Street traders. Often in the papers, leading the accused through an angry crowd.

Art walked me home, steering my elbow. He said we'd talk after I'd had time to think. I said I'd done all the thinking I was going to do. I asked for a local Realtor reference. He said nothing for a while.

"You don't want to do this, Lee."

We stood facing each other, his white Mexican shirt sloping down his chest like God's cloak. Hands in pockets. Horn-rims sparkling in sun. I tried not to cry.

"I do," I lied.

He sighed. "For many reasons, you don't."

"I need to. It's not about want. I need the money."

"Lee, I can tell you're going through a rough time. Selling a house, especially when it's the only property your mother owned, is not something you decide to do in a hurry."

"I—"

"No, you obviously have *not* considered this for very long. I can tell. What you need to do is work harder. We've all been where you are, Lee."

"I'm working as hard as—"

"Don't tell me that. I don't mean to be so rough, but I know you can swing it. You're a smart girl. Think out of the box."

"I—"

"When the going gets tough . . . you know the rest. Your mother didn't want you to sell this. It's the only heirloom she had to leave you."

"It's just a house."

"You're not going to think that in twenty years."

◇◇◇◇◇

Sunshine had drowned the yard. The light blurring the weeds reminded me of a photograph from playing cards Kai left behind.

I sifted through them sometimes, when I was talking on the phone, or getting drunk by myself, as if they had the mystical significance of tarot cards. Shot in the seventies, the pictures on the cards weren't airbrushed, the girls weren't skinny, and everything was real. A blonde on a wicker throne, pulling beige crochet bikini aside. A girl on a black couch, kneeling away from us, red bra, black bob, lavender star points of asshole. A brunette on a beach shack porch, legs spread, sand crusted on knees and shoulders, glass of white Zinfandel in her hand.

The queen of hearts was a strawberry-blonde in a golden field. Hair feathered. Grass up to her pussy. One hip forward. A black-eyed Susan to her nose. She looked like she smelled of patchouli, drank jug wine, did macramé, flew kites. She had a little belly.

I stood in my own field, wanting obligations to fall from me. This is one way of contemplating suicide, yet it's the exact opposite: what I wanted was to be alive, to escape all the damage, to shed it like snakeskin, to emerge pure and naked and laughing.

Cobalt evening in the city. A rain was falling, warm as tea water, when I got to Yves's lobby. I buzzed his loft.

"Hello?" he asked, voice doubtful.

"It's me, Yves."

A hesitation. Nothing. Then the buzzer sounded. I vaulted up three flights and waited, nervous, hair pasted to face. He opened the door wearing a silk robe and leather slippers, hair sticking up like chick's fur. When he was pissed, his eyes developed a dark dimension of blue.

"Come in, kid. You look terrible."

He put an arm around me, took my purse, put me on the white leather couch, and fixed me a scotch. I was shaking.

He helped peel off my clothes and put on his pajamas. We sat together. I touched his bottom lip with my fingertip.

"My God, you have a temper, Lee," Yves said.

"I'm an asshole," I whispered.

I scratched at his thigh while he played with the hair that fell down my back as we talked, and I noticed he was stiff under the robe. All I wanted to do was get in bed with ice cream and cigarettes, and watch cartoons, but I owed him.

I let my hand wander. He kept playing with my hair, but his motions got mechanical and messy and distracted, the way they do when a man starts to feel pleasure. I set my tumbler on the glass table and kneeled between his legs, my body flush with purpose. But as I arranged him and glanced up with the "here I go" look, he suddenly pulled the robe closed and stood, walked away.

My mother used to call me her hummingbird: that was her gentle way of saying I was hyperactive and unmanageable. She didn't try to manage me; she gave me shelter. On a winter beach, she'd open her coat to let me walk in her warmth.

I broke or misplaced anything she ever loaned me, from a pink cashmere beret I left at the Roxy coat check to a gold anklet with an aquamarine charm I lost in the ocean.

I was the child who swiped icing off the cake before it was served. I ate M&M's I'd dropped on the floor of Penn Station. When we were twelve, my friend and I served hors d'oeuvres at her parents' Christmas party, and I poured the dregs of everyone's drinks into one glass, which I drank in the laundry room.

As an infant, I'd screamed around the clock until my mother made a cradle of a white stole folded into an orange crate. She crossed her fingers. Thus buried, I slept and dreamed.

When I was a little older, I feigned sleep. Who didn't? The memory of my mother's perfumed hand pulling the sheet over my shoulder could still provoke a rush of love. I remembered lying in the dark, breathing as though dreaming, shivering at the promise of footsteps as she came down the hall to kiss me good night. The kiss was good, but that ritual of enclosure was everything.

When I was five, on the icy night of a cocktail party, I hid under the mountain of coats in the guest room. My face against a silk lining that reeked of opium and cigarettes, my hand clasping a bunch of lamb's wool that smelled of snow. I must have fallen asleep. Next thing I knew, I woke up in a darkness of fur and wool to voices of people come to get their wraps. I stared at two faces and the pink chandelier behind them. The story was repeated often, how Mary and Kirk found me buried like a stowaway. Since then, I'd rarely known refuge like that pile of coats, but I looked for it all the time.

As an adult, it was difficult to find my way into the warm lair of another person's soul. When I got to New York, I took art classes at Spring Studio. Jules had posted an anonymous request there for female models; if he'd included his name, people would pose just to get into his studio. He was in his late seventies then, and breathed like a sick dog. I adored him. I reclined on green velvet, and he let me stretch every twenty minutes. Jules talked to himself; I was caught in his dream. *Oh, yeah, she's a calendar girl. That's a decadent leg, see. She might be tired of this position.* He'd knock the brush around the water jar. *Well, let's see if blue doesn't work. We should think about the time. We should get down to the liquor store before it closes.* Even though I hadn't seen him in a few years, when I read his obituary a couple months ago, I bawled. The universe had turned another spirit out of this city, and me out of another home.

I followed Yves into the bedroom, where he was sitting on the bed, hands clasped between his knees. The bedside light spread a golden umbrella that included him from the waist down; his face was dark. I hovered on the threshold, arms crossed.

"What's wrong with you?" I asked meanly.

"I'm exhausted. I didn't sleep, worrying about you," he said. "And now you want to erase your misbehavior with what I will concede is a generous gesture but a gesture nonetheless."

"I said I was sorry," I muttered.

"I know, I know." He turned away.

Now this is strange, I decided. This man who shows emotions like a movie star is at a loss for words. A part of me wanted to walk out the door, leave a note in the kitchen, the kind of note I'd never written, or maybe no note at all.

"You should see a doctor," he said.

"Why?"

"For your health, Lee, why else. You can't take pills and drink like you do, and you can't do coke and then take those pills. You end up speaking gibberish, you know. You're a mess."

"Well, fuck you very much," I told him.

He sighed. "Can you just bite the bullet and look at yourself?"

"I look at myself all the time."

"No," he said. "You need to get it together."

"But *Yves*," I said, exasperated. "That's not who I am. I'm not together."

He pondered the floor for a while. "You can't run away like that. You can't take my car."

"Is this about me taking your car?"

"I'm only saying there has to be a line. I have to draw a line."

His eyes, blue diamonds in the gloom. I crossed the floor and sat on the bed. Then I put my arms around his body and my head to his chest. We stayed like that for a long time.

"Something has to change, Lee."

TWO

⬦⬦⬦

She stands in front of the washbasin and picks up her lipstick.
Camera pans across to her reflection as she applies it. Still
reflected in the mirror, we see her turn and pick up a brassiere
from a chair behind her. Camera tilts down as she picks up the
rest of her underwear from a stool in the foreground.

Medium shot of SEVERINE coming through a deserted
apartment, carrying her underwear. Camera pans right round
to show her from behind as she goes into the drawing room,
where a wood fire is burning. Then it tracks in as she sits down
beside the fireplace and throws her underclothes and stockings
into it; they catch fire immediately.

—from the script of *Belle de Jour*, by LUIS BUÑUEL,
on Severine's first day as a prostitute

Before bedtime, Yves ritualistically lowered shades in every room. At night, the edges of the shades glowed lavender, and in the morning, golden. He woke early and circled his loft, raising each shade. He moved slowly, as though he'd created the city in his sleep and was now unveiling it.

Tonight I slipped out of sheets, breathless, afraid of waking the light sleeper. In the living room, I raised one shade to see without turning on a light. Blue shadow beads of rain dotted the white Hermès couch. At my own house, I alleviated insomnia with PlayStation, a vibrator, warmed strawberry milk, Ambien, but all I could do here was take an ashtray and smokes to the bathroom.

My body was so dehydrated, I pissed urine like molasses. Sprayed Chanel cologne into the air for no reason. My image was repeated in black tiles like a hundred fairies. My face in the mirror: collapsed from scotch and nightmares. I stared. Ever since the day my mom told me about her lungs, a paranoia had been mounting: the outside might be fine, the inside, disaster. The image I couldn't banish was a pint of raspberries. On top the ruby berries looked juicy. Unwrapped and spilled into the colander, they revealed undersides black with rot.

Of course, two weeks had gone by and I'd ignored Anthony's warning. The previous morning, an eviction notice was stapled to my door: waking up to the noise, I thought someone was breaking in.

I lit a cigarette. I had three options.

I could move in here. But we had different ideas about housekeeping. I'd left his milk out overnight more than once. I spilled red wine on the white couch when I tried to take a sip lying down. I almost overflowed a bubble bath; he caught the foam when it was level with the rim. And while Yves kept Purex hidden in every drawer, me, if I ran out of panties, I turned a pair inside out. I brought home a Versace lipstick left in a ladies' room, and Yves stealthily pulled it out of my hands as if prying a loaded pistol from a toddler's grasp.

Or I could ask for a loan. But we never actually talked about money. It was silently acknowledged he had more, but to admit I was being sued by creditors and evicted would be humiliating. He looked aristocratic but was actually self-made.

Yves was closemouthed on his past. A business partner of his, while we were waiting for Yves at Nobu, told me Yves quit school at fifteen to work on barges. By twenty-two, he'd made his way into the buying and selling of whatever cargo the barges transported. He was soon buying and selling barges, then buying and selling the companies that owned barges.

Tucked into his humidor was a yellowed photograph with scalloped edges. A dark, bulbous car on a dirt road. The blur of a chicken. A thin boy scowled at the sky. Shadows cast by brow bones obscured his eyes. Mouth blanched from sun, making shadow under lower lip. One shoe open at the toe. His head reached the car door's handle. His hands hung neither clenched nor relaxed, but curved; this boy was precociously self-conscious. He could see the loneliness and unpleasant work required of him if he discarded his natural destiny and tried to write a new one.

Watching guests at his own parties, Yves reminded me of a cat crouched on an indoor sill, tracking starlings in the yard.

◇◇◇◇◇

When Yves walked into the bathroom, I was twisting out my eighth cigarette. He asked what I was doing.

"Selling my house," I answered, as if that were obvious.

He looked at me a moment, scratched his chest. "Start from the beginning."

"Nothing to explain."

"You're selling your house at five in the morning." Yves stepped to the mirror to push and pull his face. Then he put the toilet lid down, sat, placed one ankle on the other knee and stared at me.

"What?" I asked.

He shrugged.

After a while, my face got hot. I turned away from him.

"You're out of money," he said.

"I am not," I said, blushing.

"It's funny," he started, "I've wondered for a long time now how you were paying your rent."

"You think I'm a screw-up."

"I think you're a young woman living in a big city."

"Art, the guy who lives in the main house, said I should work harder. And he was right," I said earnestly. Then I shrugged. "What I should do is be someone else."

He actually laughed. "Art probably just doesn't want someone building on the lot." Then he looked at me and sighed. "Are you going to regret this?"

"I don't have a choice."

"How about this," he said. "I'll cover you."

Yes, he'd bought me things, taken me to dinner. And I'd plucked a twenty here, a fifty there from his wallet. If he gave me a hundred to pay for a round of drinks, I pocketed the change. But I spent that money on toys: marzipan, gold mascara, vintage *Playboys*. This transaction would put us in a different league.

"No way," I said.

"Yes." Blue eyes unwavering.

"No," I said weakly.

He smiled at the floor, amused. Looked up at me again. "Yes," he said quietly.

"I need a pretty big loan," I warned him.

"I'm not loaning you money. This is a gift."

"Yves, I can't, that's just—"

"A gift, or nothing."

We squabbled, and my refusals got less and less sincere. We sealed the deal with a kiss: closemouthed, since he didn't like sleep breath. He got up to leave as I lit the last smoke in my pack.

"One thing, though," he said. "You can't smoke like that in here, love. The towels"—he gestured at them—"absorb the smell. Let's change them tomorrow."

Broken by storm, umbrellas lay along Spring Street like birds shot from the sky. We sat in a red banquette, the earliest table. The staff was sleepy. I breathed in coffee, baking bread, cigarette smoke. Triangles of gold fell across white tablecloths. I ordered a chocolate croissant, espresso, a French 75.

"Are you all paid up now?" he asked. "How does it feel?"

"It feels amazing. I'll take this opportunity to thank you again."

"Please don't. It was my pleasure," he said.

When Yves finished, he swiped bread over yolk. Patted a napkin to his mouth. "I wonder if you could do me a favor."

I looked at him.

"There's this guy. Kelly," he said.

"Y-es," I said slowly.

"You know my friend Guy?" he asked. "The photographer?"

"I know of him."

"A good friend of his just showed up in New York. Needs a job."

"And?"

"Thought he could tend bar at the restaurant."

I made an exasperated noise. "Are you kidding? I have staff waiting for years to tend bar."

"Sorry," he said blandly. "I thought you were in charge."

"Yves," I warned.

"Look," Yves said casually, "use this guy. Abuse him. I don't care, lamb. Just pay him."

We looked at each other for a while. I detected merriment in his eyes.

I licked jam off my knife. "Not like I can say no."

He signaled for the bill. "Don't do anything you don't want to do," he said.

"Don't do anything you don't want to do," I mimicked.

"You have bad manners," he said.

"Of course I do, daddy. That's why you hang out with me."

I applied red lipstick, twisted to kiss the mirror behind us. While he extracted a credit card from his wallet, I licked my lips and pouted at the waiter.

Yves had given me more than six months' rent, but it pained me to pay my landlord in advance. At one, the Town Car showed down the block from the restaurant, and we took a tour of the neighborhood. Donald talked the whole time about a little black girl named Jenny he'd shacked up with in Miami recently.

"Magic," he kept saying. "Sugar and spice."

I told Donald he was a whore.

"Just the tiniest little body," he said reverently, "miniature bones, beautiful mouth." He gave me an extra bump on my way out the door.

Every twenty minutes, I slipped into the ladies' room. Doing drugs in the workplace was like being naked under a fur coat. The secret was half the pleasure.

I popped my cocaine cherry at a wedding when I was fifteen. I spent the reception in a hotel room with strangers who tried to plug my nosebleed and soak the blood out of my pink pantsuit. But even then, red blooming on my pants, staring past these people into an azalea-hedged parking lot full of limousines, I knew I'd do it again.

Kai lived on blow. Had to carry Neosporin to doctor his nostrils. He believed you did what you needed to succeed, and for him to go to that kitchen every night, he needed help. Hard work, luck, connections, a trust fund, and talent weren't enough, he used to say, in New York City. You needed to buy an edge here, if you found it for sale.

Drugs turned the cardboard box of an ordinary day into a honeycomb, dripping and blond. Dip into that hour, huddle in this one, buzz away with your wings wet and sweet.

Chico's bug eyes were always half lidded so he looked high when he wasn't. I teased him because he'd had his hair cut like a little boy. He wore a plaid button-down and Diesel jeans, and smiled like a saint. Our spirits were braided together by work. We'd shared rough nights, easy nights, after hours. Food, liquor, blood, sweat, tears. Even as prep cooks, we'd been kings, peeling potatoes side by side. Now we comanaged the restaurant, rarely seeing each other since we worked opposite shifts.

We sat at his kitchen table. The Chelsea apartment was tiny, and the walls were lined with shelves like a walk-in cooler. On the makeshift counter: tofu, onions, and kale on a cutting board. We drank ginger beers.

"Is this alcoholic?" I asked after my first potent sip.

"No, Lee," he said condescendingly. "It's good for you. Imagine that."

Chico's pregnant wife lay in bed in the other room, hair parted around Mickey Mouse ears. When I'd arrived and went to say hello, I put a hand on her belly and was repulsed by the tautness. I started to tell her about a hamster of mine who ate her babies, and Chico put his hands on the back of my shoulders and steered me into the kitchen. He told me I was scaring Audrey.

Across the street, on the window gates at the welfare hotel, hung magenta G-strings and baby clothes. The sun burned a bloody red, and I eventually came to my point.

"But Shannon's going to throw a fit," he said. "He's been banking on shifts behind the bar since April."

"We'll work him in, I promise."

He was swirling the liquid in the bottle. "That's not too cool, Lee."

"You think I don't know that?"

"So, what's the story? Can't you just say it's not a good idea, it's not going to work out?"

"Uh, no?"

He looked at me, arms folded across his chest. Chico, not unlike Yves, played when he wanted but had started working at the age of nine. To get out of Sunset Park, he'd paid a ransom whose terms no one else would ever know. He never put that in my face, which made his conscience all the more formidable. I blew my bangs up and swallowed my drink.

"Don't look at me like that, for Chrissakes," I pleaded after a while. "Yves gave me money. That's why. It's his friend's friend. There. Now you know."

"Lee, that's fine," he said immediately. "All you have to do is tell me this kind of thing, and we'll go from there."

"I'm going to meet the guy after this," I said glumly. "At least make sure he's not a total freak."

"Like I said. Totally fine."

"It's not fine," I argued.

Chico shook his head, looked at the ceiling. "Oh my God. Whatever."

On the way to the subway, I lit a smoke. Glanced over at La Nouvelle Justine. A man in leathers, in a contraption like a gladiator's bathing suit, was paid to squat by the door to the restaurant. He patted his shaved head like a monkey. I dropped my burning match to the sidewalk.

Across from Relish, fifteen or twenty motorcycles stood outside a repair shop, tilted on kickstands. I was early. The girl in the next booth was looking out the window but seeing something that wasn't there. I wondered if she was a retail girl, junkie, grad student, graphic designer. A temp, maybe: this city was full of kids with red marks where they usually wore nose rings, club stamps from the night before on their hands, cornered into cubicles, answering to corporate masters. I wondered if she was in love with a painter, a skinhead, a girl. I liked the way she held the burger with two hands, like a kid, unafraid of getting greasy.

It was infuriating that I had to do this. I especially hated that Yves, who acted so worldly, would do anything for someone famous. What had Guy done for Yves?

Manhattan lights were shining through the violet buildings

on this side of the river. A girl glided by in a white sundress, bony shoulders. She adjusted the bandanna holding her hair, arms glowing in the night. Her dog, unleashed, didn't stray.

A shout in the street. Two white guys greeting each other. One with mohawk and kilt, the other in overalls, carrying a canvas wrapped in brown paper.

"What's up, bitch," one thundered.

They knocked fists. Some of the kids in Williamsburg had watched *Basquiat* too many times. All the people in the gold-lit diner looked, faces reflected blue in the windows; the reflections were superimposed on the street, the chrome of bikes glinting beyond in the shadows.

I knew him the minute he walked into the place. Enormous shoulders and almond eyes. White sweatshirt cut sleeveless. Blue jeans and boots. Tattoos on the inside of both wrists. Auburn ponytail streaked by the sun. He was a little bit cowboy, a little bit Indian. As he walked to the table, he glanced around as if he'd never been in a restaurant.

"So, what's up?" I asked, going for the aggressively casual.

He shrugged. "Not too much. How are you?"

I shrugged. "What do you drink?"

"Nothing for me, thanks."

He sat with legs spread, but arms crossed. Head like a boulder, except when he lowered or raised his chin, revealing broad planes and dimensions like the subject of a Cubist portrait. Freckles, as dark as dark chocolate, speckled skin opalescent from too much sun. He stared, waiting for questions.

"You just got here?"

"I did," he answered. "I came in on a fishing charter. I was first mate."

"Sounds fancy," I said.

He smiled. "Actually, I was cutting fish open and taking their guts out."

"What are you doing in New York?"

This was his only hesitation. At the bar, a girl in a mesh shirt, angel wings of hair in her face, dried glasses with a cloth.

"I'm looking for someone," he said finally.

"Do you mean," I started, annoyed at his coyness, "someone you hope exists, or someone real?"

"She's real." He enunciated as if speaking to a child.

We discussed the restaurant, his shifts, his pay. He looked at me steadily, didn't fidget, and spoke when spoken to. I didn't buy his act. His act was that he had no act.

When we were done, he moved out of the booth and stood, hulking. He was much taller than me, and I'm tall. Reached out to shake my hand. Thanked me for meeting him.

"Just so you know," I added, "I'm hiring you as a favor to Yves. There are people who've waited for this position, who earned it, and they're going to be pissed when you walk in."

His face turned scarlet.

"Thanks for letting me know," he said.

He tucked hair behind ear and held up one hand, fingers spread like star points, a gesture that said good-bye as much as it said don't follow. Then turned and shoved the hand into his pocket, jangling the wallet chain attached to his belt loop, and walked carefully to the door.

I walked home through hot streets. Old people sat by doorways in beach chairs. Moonbeams made white garage doors creamy, as in an oil painting. I stepped around dog turds, big as soup cans, from the rotties, Dobermans, and collies. Gulls bathed in roof puddles left from a storm, heads visible over gutter pipes.

The sky made more sense here than in Manhattan, the brown dome a sparkling map of constellations. I let my eyes linger on a couple walking toward me, each carrying a bottle of red wine. She in a party dress with a thrift-store purse, he in a lime-green suit, a bleached lock of hair falling over his forehead, the rest of his hair black. Nights like this, after it rained, you'd never seen anything as beautiful as the reflection of a red stoplight on the street, or a white cat darting through the wet indigo alley behind Black Betty.

Near the BQE, garbage fluttered in the trucks' wind like confetti, except the condoms caught in glass-spangled weed, Roughriders full of custard. In a tinted-out Monte Carlo parked under the highway, the pale shape of a man's head was tipped back against the headrest, sleeping or cracked out or getting blown. You'd never seen anything so beautiful as that woman in the building across the street from me, blue-black punk hair, a man's sleeveless undershirt, black leather cuff on her wrist, smoking through the window bars, watching the night.

Fans blew hot air through my four doorless rooms.

The kitchen's high, antique tin ceiling looked down on the industrial shelves, table, and counters Kai had installed. The bathroom was closet-sized. The shower's tiles were white, except for an aqua patch that replaced tiles that had fallen when the caulking rotted. No sink; I brushed my teeth in the kitchen, spitting on dirty plates.

The second room was tiny, and since the apartment had no closets, I hung my clothes there on a garment rack. A white sequined skirt glimmering in perpetual darkness. Cardboard boxes of shoes. A full-length mirror. Gold bangles on the dusty floor.

The third room was larger, painted midnight blue. TV and stereo on the floor, orange butterfly chair, books in piles. Corona bottles on the television. Video games, record albums, empty packs of cigarettes scattered so it was hard to walk through the room.

Blue beads hung between that room and the bedroom, painted Chinese red. My sheets smelled of booze, smoke, dreams. A yellow lantern stood on the bedside table, illuminating lipstick and powder and kohl pencils. This way, I could put on makeup, looking into a Hello Kitty hand mirror, before I got out of bed.

For three years, Kai and I gave dinner parties every week.

A Polaroid still nailed to the wall: dark kitchen, candles, Kai's paella, champagne Jill lifted from the cellar where she worked. Crowded around the table, a motley crew, arms around one another. David's blond mullet standing up like a rooster tail. Belinda, with a fedora on her white hair, sticking out her tongue. Jack's muscles cut, tattooed, displayed in cutoff cowboy shirt. Deedee still in chef clothes, straight from work. Jill and Ali in vintage dresses, the floral prints reminiscent of curtains in Midwestern motels.

After he'd left, I sanded the floor. I burned incense. I threw out everything Kai forgot. Sometimes, I still spotted a local crackhead in Kai's baby-blue tux shirt. I invited friends over one night and made mojitos. It felt strange to be the sole host. We got drunk, ordered food from the Dominican place on the corner, turned up the stereo, and danced. We fell asleep, three of us on the bed, one in the chair, and a pair on the floor, nestled in their coats, as the sun rose milky and pink in my windows. I never had people over again.

In my solitude, then, I did a lot of thinking. I'd been waiting for some oasis to open where there was time for love, art, booze, paychecks, and sleep. Perhaps this was a slightly unrealistic expectation. All my life, first the idea and then the reality of this city had been my fuel. At some point, the tables had turned, and the city was using me for inspiration. Too bad my lifeblood was just a drop in New York's tanks. So one night, I wrote a plan for change and was loyal to it for a couple months.

The agenda included dragging out my white faux-alligator briefcase in which I kept brushes and paint. At Pearl I bought missing items like turpentine and cadmium yellow. Ate cereal for dinner in the name of health and budget. If I went out, I came home after one drink. If I worked late, at least I gessoed and toned a couple canvases before I got in bed. If work was slow, I sketched preliminary studies on the backs of liquor invoices. My mother started to need me more, and I spent hours on the train, trying not to think, drawing in a black book. I waited for this new lifestyle to stop feeling false and robotic, but that sensation only got worse.

One evening I was jogging, and stopped to pant. A mirrored storefront reflected my red Pumas splattered with paint, my pink terry-cloth shorts, the rope of gold chains I never took off, and the hives on my thighs from exertion. My face was mauve. *Trying to be normal,* I thought, *is turning me into more of a freak.*

Now the kitchen was crammed with pizza boxes, vodka bottles. Fruit flies feeding off a peach pit in the sink. Overfull ashtrays in every room. Canvases jammed under the bed. I sat on my floor, looking at my home. And I loathed it. Ironic how I was fighting to stay there.

◇◇◇◇◇

On Monday, when I got to the restaurant, Kelly was sitting at the bar in the uniform of jeans, white shirt, tie. Outside, it was one of those late-summer days when everything looks as if it were dipped in maple syrup.

Our waitstaff, mainly boys, hustled. They made money by being charming, by seeming eager. They nursed orphanage dreams: rich couple drives up in glossy car, the man supporting the mysteriously bereft woman's elbow, and they scan the dirty faces until their eyes lock on you.

Ozzie lived on an unheated floor of a sweatshop off the tenth Brooklyn L stop. Martine lived in Chelsea with his grandmother, whom he supported. Josh moved around, brought his backpack to work, brushed his teeth in the men's room.

Toothaches, manic depression, strep throat. No health insurance: these kids doctored themselves with Aleve and microwaved brandy. I once gave Shannon cash because he had crabs. I'm not maternal, but he had tears in his eyes. They were sweet and desperate kids, and I expected them to dislike Kelly.

"Morning," I said.

"Good morning." Kelly was eating a mango. Staring. Waiting for me to break down and be nice.

I introduced him to the staff. When everyone dispersed, Kelly hucked the end of the fruit into the garbage, rinsed his hands. Quietly, he asked if I was at least going to give him a chance. I pretended I hadn't heard.

I called Donald. I jumped from the hot street into the cold car, then back into the hot street.

To me, drugs radiated light, like holy crumbs. All day I wandered the restaurant with coke in my pockets, certain the stuff was glowing through the fabric.

Once, I fumbled and lost a hit of E on the Tunnel dance floor, but a shaft of light shined up at me from between all those shoes. I bent to retrieve the capsule with religious grandeur.

Even my handbag changed when there were drugs inside it. It became heavier and more important, more elegant. All I had to do was look at my dresser, and I knew which drawer to open. When introduced to people, I saw auras, a purple haze of antidepressant, the gold chain mail of Demerol.

I got quiet whenever I met a new medicine cabinet at a party. I looked at my reflection, then opened the door stealthily, as though birds might rush out.

In Yves's loft, I dropped my purse on the floor. Kicked off heels. I swayed, unsteady, and lit a smoke.

We'd gone to the World Financial Center orchid show, the tall glass building lush with magenta throats, green pods, freckled yellow tongues of petal. Then we had martinis upstairs at the Hudson River Club. Many martinis. Just enough martinis for me to tell him.

I chased olives around with a pick. "I spent it all."

He looked at me for a long time, but I wouldn't look up. So he'd taken out his checkbook right there at the bar.

"I feel like Heidi Fleiss," I whispered conspiratorially, even passionately, thinking that the second time had been easy, even exciting.

But now I felt like shit.

Something scuffled on the floor. Yves walked into the living room, snapped on the light. Hurried after it. Snapped on the kitchen light: the bird strutted under the butcher-block table.

"C'mere, birdie," Yves said, crouching and approaching. "Don't be afraid."

"I bet he's got rabies."

"He's just scared. Birds don't have rabies, Lee."

The pigeon launched itself at Yves, boomeranged off his shoulder, fluttered around the loft. Yves started to chase it. Somehow, the gray bird found its way back to the fire escape window, which was open a foot, and burst out.

Yves, panting, walked stiffly to the bar.

"You okay?"

He poured a glass. Sipped. "Yes," he said in a steely voice.

"Are you getting geriatric on me?" I said.

He gave me a hard look.

It was a stormy night, and half the reservations had bailed. Kelly read *Mr. Boston* in his California lilt.

"Yo," he said to no one in particular, turning stained pages. "Check this out. 'Golden Cadillac. Cream, OJ, crème de cacao, Galliano.' Nice."

He flipped pages.

"'Wedding Bells. OJ, gin, Dubonnet, cherry brandy.' That's lovely, that really is. Sweet."

Martine, Vanessa, and Josh sat at the bar as if their favorite uncle was telling a bedtime story. I eavesdropped as he displayed his tattoos: on one wrist, Black Flag lyrics his friend had inked into his skin with a needle when they were sixteen, and on the other, a honeysuckle blossom he'd had done in Amsterdam. No one else could see through this guy. He acted humble and innocent, and got everything he wanted. When he had a break, he jotted notes in a spiral notebook that was falling apart. He was playing the intellectual, the poet, the vagabond, the beggar. But he was just an interloper.

I couldn't even depend on Shannon, although he held out the

longest. He could be a prick, in general. Tall and skinny, with a long face, wireless glasses, dishwater-blond hair he wore in a ponytail. Chinese star tattooed in green on neck.

Shannon made a point of ignoring Kelly, even knocking into him when he unloaded glasses behind the bar. But at the end of last night, in the kitchen, a couple busboys huddled around the two men. Shannon held an oyster in his fingertips. He shrugged like a boxer. Then snorted it.

"That," Kelly said, arms folded, "was magnificent."

And Shannon blushed.

Belinda called the next morning to invite me to dinner.

"C'mon," she said. "Matt, Jane, and I just got back from Miami. I haven't seen you in forever."

"I'm so busy; I'm overwhelmed."

"How's your work? Are you painting?"

"More than ever," I lied.

Against my intuition, I agreed to come over Wednesday of the following week.

The last time I'd been in Miami was with Belinda, three years ago. Delano lobby at two in the morning. Celestial curtains hung from the ceiling, and Belinda and I walked through this luscious dream. Two men approached, asked if we had dates. We didn't know what that meant in Miami, so we coyly said no.

Sapphire sky, black windows of cubic buildings painted chalk or banana or rose. Junkies and runaways waltzed through the streets. The night air hot with wrongdoing. The men walked us to another bar. We stopped at an all-night drugstore for cigarettes. The citizens of Miami, God love them, reminded me of children who weren't too bright, who'd grown up in thin-walled houses where they had to hear their parents fuck and fight. These kids walked around the drugstore wired, dazed, and drunk, their golden toxic bodies statues of debauchery.

Over gimlets, my guy finally popped the question: How much?

"Excuse me?" I'd said.

"What do you charge?" he asked.

The past couple hours were torn backward, like film ripped through a projector. Nothing had been what I'd thought it was. I leaned to Belinda, deep in earnest conversation with her guy.

"Yo," I said, tugging at her skirt. "They think we're hookers."

She laughed all night while we lay on our hotel beds, watched Leno, ate candy from the minibar. I tried to take it as lightly, since that's what we were good at doing. But some part of me stood accused by the mix-up.

A wet day. I spent half my shift at the window, arms crossed, watching rain pound the street, pound the purple Japanese maple leaves, the yellow awning with red lettering: CANDY CIGARETTES NEWSPAPER COLD SODA.

Martine slunk in an hour late. Tendrils of wet black hair on his forehead. Almost a foot shorter, he had to look up at me: violet and apricot bruises around one eye.

"What's up, Spuds MacKenzie," Ozzie greeted him, grinning around the tub of dishes on his shoulder.

Martine continued his hangdog stare. I suppressed a smile, asked what happened.

"Tried to get on someone's girl," Josh said, without looking up from the espresso machine.

Martine turned at him. "I didn't know," he spat.

Later, I lit a cigarette at the bar, the boys turning chairs onto tables. Lights extinguished.

Those orchids from the other night hung in my head, a mobile turning in a dark nursery, me looking up from my crib as they spun lazily. Ghostly toys of lavender and ivory, a hot perfume shed from them like dust, like the particles of sex.

And then Martine's face joined the vision, cheekbones blued and yellowed in circular shapes—the paisley bruises symbolizing desire.

And all of it was fused, suddenly, into a man's face filigreed with orchid petals, the pistil of an eyelash dropping pollen, sulky mouth the red lip of flower, periwinkle skin. This three-dimensional bust loomed in my mind.

I did want to paint. But for some time now, whenever I committed details to a cocktail napkin, the heart of the idea stopped beating.

I inherited this halfway syndrome from my mother. At five two, my mother weighed a hundred pounds soaking wet. Her simian face was playful, her orange curls innocent, but she wouldn't have been, and wasn't, caught dead without lipstick. She was half child, half woman. She'd light up after crushing a half-smoked cigarette and never waited to finish a drink before she refreshed it. She slept on the couch and ate in bed. She could never fall asleep and always slept late.

No one could help loving her. Guests would arrive at eight and find her in a damp bikini, only beginning to scour cookbooks for ideas. But the night would be unforgettable: midnight dinner on the porch, an impromptu reading of *A Midsummer Night's Dream*, children playing in the rhododendrons—their bodies illusory as vapors. She never read the books for the book club, and missed most meetings, but when it was her turn to host, she warmed the winter afternoon by serving hot cider and gingersnaps and jazz. The girls laughed, gossiped, and forfeited the book. In the community center dressing room, my mother painted on a geisha face. Her kimono belt was wet from the toilet, and there weren't enough bobby pins to secure her wig, but she cracked deadpan joke after joke till the cast was crying, literally, dabbing white makeup with tissue. On stage, she froze, but she made that backstage room, with its mirrors and hot lights and cheap costumes, into theater.

Too many unconsummated plans, though. Dead dogwood saplings leaning against the house, roots trapped in burlap sacks, unplanted. Yellowing patterns and fabric for dresses never sewed. A white upright with a bench full of unlearned standards. She'd half loved men, and they'd half failed her. Combing my hair with her fingers, when one had finally left after dinner, she explained how he'd have made a great husband but a bad father, or vice versa. Even I could be counted among her unfinished dreams. I was not anything. I was an incomplete work. She died quickly, but not peacefully. She fought like someone caught in the doors of an elevator.

I believe, in fact, she lived her whole life caught between the fifties and the sixties, stranded between convention and freedom. Stuck between what she was supposed to be and what she wanted to be.

My mom took me to meet my grandfather only once, even though he lived in New Jersey. At ten, I'd just had my first growth spurt, and while we waited on his stoop, my mom told me to pull my rabbit-fur jacket over my belly. The ice on the steps was studded with rock salt. A bird feeder, empty of seed, dangled from the eave.

"Well, well," he said, as I'd imagined he would, and he shook my mitten.

The living room was shrouded in plastic, even though the dog had died years ago. The visit had been planned for lunchtime, but he offered none. Although the lamps were off, a powerful whiteness that fell short of actual light came through the window from the snow outside.

I don't remember why we went, or what they talked about. I probably slouched on the sofa, fiddling with my jacket zipper, staring at him through narrowed eyes. His lips were full and red, and a blueprint for mine, but I found them repulsive on a six-foot-three man with a white crew cut.

"Glad that's over, little partner," my mom said in the car, her hand searching for my fries.

"What's wrong with him?" I asked.

She squinted, thinking. The turnpike's shoulder was a gray wall of snow. I unwrapped my steaming cheeseburger from its paper. When I was older, she'd explain that she left home at eighteen because her dream was to be an actress, which he insisted was prostitution. They'd fought violently about many things over the years, but that had been the breaking point.

"Hmmm," she said now, hoping to explain this to a ten-year-old. "The problem is, he fears being moved. He hates anything that moves him."

She darted a glance at me. I looked up, unaffected, from removing pickles.

"What that means, Lee," she continued, "is he doesn't like to be made to feel anything. He doesn't like pleasure or sorrow or joy or anger unless he's chosen it, unless he controls it. He doesn't like when someone expresses herself. It makes him feel dirty."

She lit a cigarette, replaced the glowing lighter, cracked the window.

"Tell me if this makes you cold, baby," she said, simultaneously exhaling smoke into cold air.

Like I said, we only visited him once. He didn't know where we lived, and I doubt he ever left his house, but I think he visited my mother all the time.

When Yves inquired about Kelly's performance, I told him the guy was a bit off, seemed to think he was above it all.

"So, you've traveled a lot?" I asked Kelly one day. "Where've you been?"

He was wiping the bar. "Wow. I think it would be easier to say where I haven't been."

Then, after waiting a beat, he looked up and smiled. And that was it.

The staff used to drink at Liquor Store Bar after closing, and they always invited Kelly.

"Cool," he'd say. "Maybe I'll join you guys."

But he'd slip out before we assembled.

He seemed blank, like a teenage boy in calculus class: he'd learned to fake an attentiveness that would keep him out of any spotlight.

Once in a while, he relaxed, and then he had a lazy smile. He'd slouch on a stool, or against the bar, pelvis tilted, legs loosely crossed. If he was happy, his big cheeks flushed and shone.

"Want a dried papaya?" he'd ask me, or anyone around him, as he wriggled two big fingers into a plastic bag of fruit.

He ate pecan halves, bananas, trail mix. But he came in one hot day with a chocolate sundae in a paper cup. He offered everyone a bite. I watched him eat. He put whipped cream and chocolate sauce in his mouth, then flipped the plastic spoon over and pulled it out. It was the gesture of a hedonist.

I just didn't get him.

⬦⬦⬦⬦

I walked from the restaurant to Belinda's house. The first sign of fall was a change in the light. The sky threw down handfuls of gold coins, but they never landed.

Unlike her old Avenue B roof with its broken, mildewed office chairs and Astroturf and dog shit, this Tribeca terrace was bricked, hedged by lemon trees in planters. Matt was a model. Not too bright, but successful, and by far the best man she'd ever known. He was flipping fish on the grill. I pulled my sweater around me, since it was getting cold these days after sundown. Now that I was here, she didn't want to talk.

"Remember that night we got locked up on the roof with those guys from Iran? You left the keys—"

"Oh, yeah," she remembered. "We had a jug of something. Of whiskey, I think."

"That was so funny. And I wanted to climb down the side of the building. I would be dead right now."

"Yeah," she said.

"Remember when we had that huge fight," I said, "about cutting up a pill."

"Cutting a pill?"

"Cutting it in half. To share. You said it was impossible to tell where the drugs were. They weren't uniformly, uh, distributed. You made me crush it."

She looked out over the nightscape. "Oh."

Belinda fed Jane, and I finished my eighth glass of wine. By the time the moon was high, our dirty plates next to our wooden chairs, I wanted to go home.

"I'm exhausted," I said, trying to sound casual and to enunciate at the same time.

Belinda said, "Exhausted? You're wired out of your mind. Your jaw's been grinding since you got here."

I was too shocked to speak, not by what she said, but by her tone of voice. Jane was sleeping in her lap, one foot poking from the blanket.

"Do you remember, sugar," Belinda continued, "seeing me at Pastis a couple weeks ago? I can't imagine you would because you could hardly walk and it took you five minutes to recognize me."

"Seriously, Belinda, if you're about to give me a speech, you, of all people—"

"Not a speech. Not at all. I just want to know if you're all right."

I almost said, *Look at me*, then decided against it.

"We both love you," said Matt, but I didn't even turn to him.

"Have you ever thought of cutting down, sweetheart?" she asked. "I mean, simply, have you ever thought of saying no?"

"No," I said, and laughed, and slapped my knee.

"What about your own work?" she asked.

"What work?" I said.

"Exactly."

"What the hell do you mean, *exactly*?" I asked.

"What I mean is, what are you doing?"

"What, are you born-again or something? What the hell happened to you?"

I left abruptly and caught a look between them as I departed down the hallway. Slumped in the backseat, glaring at the steel web of the bridge above me, I wished things upon her that I cannot even mention here.

◇◇◇◇◇

Two men had finished dinner and were drinking at the bar. Kelly had already served them a couple drinks each, on top of what they drank at their table. The blond was big as a quarterback and young, but his nose was already gin-blossomed. The other was small and feral, hands jingling pockets, one hand darting out when he sipped his drink, then back. They hadn't taken their suit jackets off, or loosened their ties. It was as if they could minimize the drunkenness by remaining buttoned up.

Vanessa stalked up to Kelly, her eyes red with anger, holding the men's check. She pointed at it, whispered something to Kelly, and glared at the men.

The quarterback was gesturing expansively, his ash inches long, when Kelly butted in.

He stood, head down, hands in pockets. The office phone rang, and I let it.

"Who do you think you are?" I asked.

He acted like a big dog come to be kicked. White shirt unbuttoned to reveal T-shirt underneath, necktie in hand. Jeans sagged, revealing pale skin against tanned skin above, like the white belly of a shark.

"No one does that," I said. "You do not chastise a customer."

"I'm sorry, Lee. It was a mistake."

"The men had *overtipped* her. Vanessa took a seven for a one, didn't even look at the total."

"A complete mistake."

"Guess what, Dirty Harry?" I said. "You're fired."

He looked up, the whites of his eyes wet in the light. I gave him his pay in cash.

"You're wired," he said evenly.

"I am not."

"Yes. You are."

"Get out."

I knew it was wrong. I even smiled in that weird way I couldn't control when my mother used to yell at me. The city crashed and whirled around the room, and we stayed silent, a pair of bodies absorbing the blow of my decision, and then he turned and walked.

From what I could tell, there were six of them, a forever-changing cast of Israeli boys, all pale as cream with curly black hair. Their mail, which I often examined since all mail for the building came through the front-door slot, was never personal. They lived on the first floor and crookedly hung blankets for curtains, so I usually could see in. Their loft was cluttered with folding screens and junk antique chairs, an aquamarine fan with a white blade. They sat around and smoked joints, burned incense, played guitar. Sometimes they piled out of a white van, sheepish, beautiful as maidens.

Coming home that night, I heard no conversation from their barred windows. Darkness. The blanket had fallen from the rod. A young and scrawny one was sleeping on the bed right under the window. Legs and arms twisted, definitely drunk. Stripped to tighty-whities for the street to see. The bumps on his spine throwing blue shadows on his back. Bob Dylan whining. Ashtray on the sill. I reached in through the bars, brushed his cheek.

He looked up, eyes bloodshot, half lidded.

"Pull your sheet up, baby," I said.

"What?" he groaned.

"Everyone can see you."

◇◇◇◇◇

My boarding school was in rural Massachusetts, and its art studios looked onto fields of tall grass. The sports program was
dinky, but we had all the linseed oil an art student could desire. Of a population of freaks, an elite corps spent its days in
those rooms. We played mixes on the paint-speckled radio, Doc
Martens kicked off, heels of woolen-socked feet propped on the
lower bars of a stool. One minute it was early afternoon, the
palette's colors distinct and pure. The next minute, the fields
were lit by the blue fire of evening, the shoulders ached, the
palette was destroyed. In the winter, we wore coats while we
painted and flirted in the ethereal light of the snow. If someone
got cookies in the mail, the parcel was immediately divided up.
We earnestly consulted one another on whether or not a piece
was finished.

But college was different. It was everything I'd wanted and
should never have gotten. I skipped all lectures and crammed the
day before tests. I started going to Dart Night at the local pub.
My roommate taught me to do bong hits using a gas mask, the
eyes black with resin. We went to house parties where people
set things on fire and had sex in the laundry room. Granted, I'd
misbehaved in high school, but it was only in fits and starts, and
always relegated to somewhere outside the walls of the school.
Now we went camping in the Adirondacks and missed a week
and a half of classes, and no one noticed I'd been gone. I hung
out at the local coffee shop and drank cup after cup with the
skateboarders.

The art studios there were silent. No music allowed. People
pretended to wash their brushes in the sink just to look at your
easel. The first semester, almost all we did were chiaroscuro

studies of wooden blocks. I'd often turn my cafeteria grilled cheese black from the omnipresent charcoal on my fingertips.

The instructor wore shapeless black clothes and white socks under black sandals. Her salt-and-pepper hair was long and unruly, almost obscuring her John Lennon glasses. Finally I summoned the courage to show her what I'd been doing privately. I brought the canvases to her office after class. The three-foot-by-foot-and-a-half full-body portraits were on white backgrounds. There was a track star, a prom queen, a gay boy, a girl nerd. Their figures were outlined carefully but were barely filled out in patches of candy colors and dirt colors, unfinished, like Kitaj's painting of the foot soldier.

She looked for a few minutes, pressing her lips with her thumb. "They just don't reach me," she offered, gesturing. "They don't touch me."

She kept talking, but I couldn't hear her.

The day after, she came to my easel. "I hope I wasn't too hard on you," she said.

"No, of course not," I answered.

She gave me a long, inquisitive look, but I stared blindly at my work, eyes burning with hatred.

By the end of that first semester, I was on academic probation. By the end of the year, I knew I didn't want to come back. My Cape Cod plan was risky, but my mother believed in it, and so did I, and for a year, it worked: I supported myself and lived as an artist.

At work, I'd take a break from scrubbing the shower stall, lie down on the motel room bed, and look around. Wearing my yellow rubber gloves, I sketched hand-washed lingerie drying on chairs, paperbacks with red-foil embossed titles, a pink comb on the maroon carpet. When I went home at night, I turned the sketches into paintings.

I lived with Jeremy, my college roommate's older brother, and a girl named Megan in a big, shabby house in the cheap part of town; it was rented from an old couple who'd moved to Florida, and the rooms were overstuffed with their knickknacks.

My housemates were creative and solitary. Megan was into silk-screening. She was a big girl with enormous breasts, and she actually enjoyed hanging our laundry on the clothesline. Jeremy was a kitchen boy, pale and anxious. He played Joy Division and worked on sci-fi paintings of robot deer, sun gleaming on their metal flanks, and fields of cactus plants with glowing pink blossoms. A mechanical butterfly swooping by the moon. A bare-breasted woman with white-fur boots and a titanium caveman club, indigo mist obscuring her landscape.

We spent time alone on our own projects more than we spent time together. Sometimes I'd recognize a vague strain as blindness; I'd worked for hours into darkness. I'd discover I was ravenous. Sometimes Jeremy and I convened in the kitchen, starving, and made meat cereal: ground chuck and onions cooked in a pan and eaten with a spoon from a bowl. I ate tomatoes like fruit. Dinner might consist of four hard-boiled eggs consumed while standing over the sink. Once I drank chicken broth from the can because I was so hungry I thought I'd faint, my stomach too tight to accept solids.

But for financial reasons, a prep cook from Jeremy's restaurant moved in after the first year, and suddenly we were living in a house of kitchen folk. Bedrooms and basement teeming with bad ideas. They were roamers. Most had left home at fifteen or so, and in their hearts, they were forever homeless, no matter where they lived. Most had warrants out for stupid mistakes. Vegans and acidheads. They had two modes: neutral and destructive. I don't believe they meant to break everything all the time, but they were built to do so. A surreal contrast existed between the switchblades and empty Vivarin boxes and the doilies and needlepointed pillows.

This is when things got crazy. This is when I got fired from the motel and started bussing tables at a seafood place. This is when joie de vivre started to mutate into mania. This is when I started painting less and less often, with less and less passion. Big Megan checked out. Jeremy slipped through the cracks. Suddenly it was me and a herd of anarchists playing house.

I have a photograph of two skinheads in the kitchen. In the background, brown tiles with yellow daisies. The black boots look ominous on the linoleum. Mike D. bends to light a cigarette from the stove, and Mikey N. holds up a lobster oven mitt whose tip is on fire. He smiles, waving at the camera.

THREE

◇◇◇◇◇

But there were no words. I had to pray, to say some things; there was a prayer in me like an egg. But there were no words.

—JOHN FANTE, from *The Road to Los Angeles*

We sat in the Le Jardin Bistro backyard. Candlelight reflecting off the leafy trellis turned Yves's hair green. On each table, autumn roses were so lush that petals fell as I watched. The blossoms cast pink and red shadows on skin.

As Yves talked, I thought back to a high school trip to Paris. We had seen the hookers at Pigalle from a tour bus: white boas, magenta go-go boots, black eyeliner. Their reflections undulated on wet pavement. Even as teenagers, we knew what they were. It wasn't the fake pearls, or the toy-sized purses, or the standing in the rain. Musk came off them, atoms like pheromones, particles that could pass through steel.

Plenty of women reek of love, but the minute you get paid, everything changes. The taste of your kiss changes. The silk of your lingerie changes. When you walk down a sidewalk, the meaning of the street corner changes.

"This is the last place in the city my mom and I ate together," I lied, just to make trouble. "She loved it here."

He looked up from his menu, leaned forward. "I hope being here doesn't upset you."

"It might," I said, looking around. "I can't tell yet."

He looked around as well, then at me, until I shrugged.

"Oh, well," I said, opening my menu. "Never mind. What am I going to eat? I'm sick of eating."

Going out to eat was the backbone of our relationship. Until recently, if anything was wrong, all we had to do was enter the creamy churchlike calm of Chanterelle, or the black-lacquer disco of Nobu, and within moments we'd be in love again. While he read through Montrachet's bible of wines, even though he knew it by heart, I simply radiated in my chair. I was a figure from a religious painting, gold shards of light shooting from my head. Ours was an infinity of contentment: I loved being taken out, he loved making me happy, I knew he loved to make me happy more than anything, so I was happy that I'd pleased him, and so on.

But tonight I was nervous, as if on a first date. "How come we never do anything besides go to dinner?"

"It's all you ever want to do, Lee."

"Well," I said, straightening silver, "I'm getting fat."

"For Christ's sake," he muttered, staring at the tablecloth.

"Did I tell you I fired that friend of Guy's?" I confessed.

Then he sat up straight. "Are you kidding? What is *with* you, Lee?"

I smiled.

"You have become antagonistic," he pronounced.

"You can't buy me, you know."

"Stop being theatrical." His hand tore cash from his wallet, pressed it on the table. He spoke quietly. "We're taking a break, Lee. We are not going to see each other for a while. Do you understand?"

"Good," I said as he stood to leave.

"No, it's not good. You need to do some thinking. Straighten yourself out."

"Aren't you going to kiss me good-bye?" I asked as he threaded through tables.

"Think about your work," he turned back to say. "Your life."

"Are you angry, Yves?"

That night, sleepless in my bed, I tantalized myself with ideas of suicide. Ideas like the white lace-up stilettos, or the black whip, or the red teddy I owned: I wasn't into this stuff, it wasn't pretty, it wasn't me, I forgot how I'd come to own it, I would never wear it or use it, but I simply could not bring myself to throw it out.

⬦⬦⬦⬦

Monday was the first chilly evening of autumn. I was still stunned, head spinning. After work, I didn't know what to do, so I wandered. I ate a slice at the corner of Thompson and Spring, then walked, hands in pockets, wind blowing open my violet coat. I clicked along the sidewalk in black boots with tiny spike heels. Stopped to watch a gold-painted mime. He called to someone faraway, then cupped hand to ear.

At Florent, I ordered coffee and a slice of midnight cake at the counter. I was alone, and I looked around at people, looked too long into the eyes of strangers.

After my coffee, I nursed a snifter of Baileys, milk glazing the ice cubes. I hung my coat on the rack to indicate permanence and looked at my face in the mirror above the bottles of liquor. The cool air had pinked my mouth. The night had fallen quickly, the world hurrying to end itself, like I often did, rushing to darkness.

Eventually a tall gangly man, who'd been meeting my gaze in the mirror, slid stool to stool till he was sitting next to me. His head was shaved but for a fuzz of blond. His whiskey drink, which he dragged down the counter, left a wet trail.

He opened his newspaper. His voice gravelly, tremulous: "What's your sign, little lady?"

"Taurus. Can't you tell?"

He grunted, making a smile out of the wrinkles in his face. Scanned the page with knobby finger. Black dirt under nail. He started to read.

"To be candid," I interrupted, "I don't give a shit about my horoscope. If you want to talk to me, buy me a drink."

He pulled out his pockets to indicate he had no money. I laughed at him, bought him a new whiskey, and we sat companionably, like two hoboes.

⬦⬦⬦⬦⬦

Bade good-bye to my lunch-counter friend at 2:00 AM. I ambled to the Eighth Avenue L, shadowed by a transvestite in gold lamé shorts, Burberry trench. Maroon scars shining on legs.

"Beautiful night," she purred, and other niceties, one lady to another. Seeking civility, humanity, at this dark hour.

Clip-clop, high heels on cobblestones, her calf muscles knotting, kneecaps working, like a horse.

"Sweet dreams, sister," she eventually growled lovingly, and fell behind, releasing me to my own future.

Before descending into the station, I turned back. Her burnished figure lost to the clutter of brick, steam, tar, graffiti. But then, a wink of starlight: peering into compact mirror, she fingered her bangs.

How did they do it, those writers who drank all night at the bar, bought cigarettes and coffee at the deli and joked with the two Pakistani guys, flirted with the lady cop on the corner, then went home, rolled a page into the typewriter, and made prose? Or the photographers who went through their days with a camera slung around their neck? Distilling the city in the image of two boys making out on the subway, or an old woman peering at the sun? It was a miracle to me that anyone spliced work and life.

If I could only invent a machine that transcribed my dreams without reducing them to the literal. This problem reminded me of a newspaper story my mother clipped about a man in Maine. He'd handcrafted a boat in his basement. The mahogany hull alone took three years. Only when finished did he realize it would be impossible to get it out.

⬦⬦⬦⬦⬦

To get up to the Stock Exchange Luncheon Club, my handbag had to be X-rayed. The guards and I looked at skeletons of lip gloss, tampons, keys. The market had just closed, and the back bar was a madhouse. Red-faced men yelled, one hand in cashews, the other clutching highball. Ancient white-jacketed waiters tottered with trays through the forest of gilded columns.

"Whassup, lovergirl," Jamie said in her Bayside accent. She pointed at a seat. "Cheer me up. I lost money today."

"Your losing money was probably more lucrative than my making money."

Jamie and I met on the ladies' room line at Cheetah, years ago. We'd almost had a fistfight because one of us cut the other, but we ended up friends. Leaning against the sink counter, we'd spent much of that night talking about men and comparing lipsticks.

"So Yves dumped you, you dumped Yves, what?" she asked.

"What do you mean?" I asked.

"You never call me unless you're lonely."

"We're taking a break, that's all," I answered.

"Who fucked up, you or him?"

I stuttered innocently.

"Baby," Jamie said, holding my jaw maternally, "you never do nothing right."

Kevin was headed over. Only five four, he spiked his ocher hair to look taller.

"To what do we owe the pleasure?" he asked, cartilage working as he pumped gum.

"I've been dumped," I told him.

"Kevin, don't get her started," Jamie said. "She'll talk about herself all night."

"I will not!" I said. "It's just that I've never been let go without—"

"Shut up," Jamie said calmly.

◇◇◇◇◇

Our big group strolled from Broad Street to West Street, voices bouncing in the canyon between platinum buildings. The financial district was lit up bright as a room. At Morton's, our waiter rolled out the cart. He sniffed, displayed one saran-wrapped cut of meat after another. When he raised the lobster, it snapped a claw at us.

The conversation was raucous, but I was distracted by a handsome man in a sharp suit sitting to our right. His head was bald, and his cufflinks were the gold helmets of Vikings. The night did have a mythic quality. And for dessert, Lady Godiva cake, which had a powdered-sugar stencil of a woman on horseback on top and bled molten chocolate when broken open with a fork.

I laid a twenty, probably a tenth of what I owed, on the white tablecloth as a gesture. Billy and Kevin told me to put it away, as though I'd embarrassed them.

"You never heard of an expense account, Lee?"

As it often happened, we ended up at VIPs. The boys charged pink cash on their credit cards. We draped ourselves on black chairs, talked loudly. Whites of eyes, teeth, ice cubes phosphorescent in low light.

Gary sponsored a lap dance for me, and I picked the star, a Russian blonde. Down went the Lycra dress, her hand balanced on my shoulder as she picked the scrap of fabric off the Lucite spike of her shoe. White hair thrown into my face, trailed down, nails scratching my thighs. Her pink-rhinestone thong embedded like a permanent jewel.

The strippers at Baby Doll's, those girls were doomed. Dancing on a stage made from industrial carpet stapled to raw lumber, they nodded off, forgot they were stripping. Strawberry mullets, track marks on their necks.

But strippers like this Russian seemed to exist beyond the barbed wire of any society. Her blue eyes looked into mine, but she wasn't home. Floating in a starry sky, she was the Tinker Bell of the city.

The next morning, the chef sent me to the wholesale restaurant stores on the Bowery to buy a mixer. The world was hollow and gold. Light shot off the chrome of parked cars, but the kids bouncing a basketball in the street wore zipped jackets.

On the sidewalk, an ice-cream counter, haphazard as if dropped from the sky. Glass grubby from children's hands, but tubs obviously empty. Placards still told flavors—Tahitian vanilla, mint, watermelon sorbet—like a eulogy for summertime.

That night, the owner smiled once he'd closed the office door. Brendan looked like Jack Niklaus on crack, khakis pulled too tight across groin. With an almost-finished cigarette stuck between his big white teeth, he grimaced against the smoke in his eyes as he uncorked a sherry bottle and poured two glasses.

"So, what up, babe? What be happening?"

"Oh, the usual, you know, just—"

"So I got a letter from the old IRS," he told me, bending his features into a look of concern. "Looks like they want to garnish your wages."

I had a vision of my paycheck impaled on a red plastic sword with two pearl onions. "Must be a mistake," I lied.

"That's what I assumed."

I lit my cigarette elaborately, and nodded and gestured

vaguely. "I can have that taken care of immediately," I lied, when I exhaled. "I just need to call my accountant."

"Can I?" he asked, stubbing his cigarette out and indicating my pack. I knew he had his own in the drawer.

"Of course," I said emphatically. "You don't have to ask."

"Well, I just won't do anything; I'll put them off till you have it figured out," he said, sipping his drink.

"Thanks."

"You know what I think? I think maybe we each need an ice cube. This is pretty syrupy."

He looked meaningfully at me until I went upstairs for ice.

I crossed under the BQE, dust hanging in late sun. The pavement smelled sweetly of human urine. I stepped around condoms, rainwater rainbowed with gasoline, bottles. A man sat in lotus position, needle between toes. Most junkies who lived under there were white, hair greenish-gray with oil. But one, an emaciated Sammy Davis Jr., slept now on a lavender mattress, matchstick limbs clutching dirty baby blanket to his torso.

A girl trailed me, walking as though stricken with cerebral palsy: one crooked arm stuck to her chest, bunched fingers thumping her sternum. Lips turned out like a baby blowing bubbles. In the shadows under the highway, her skin glowed. A gash down her forehead stitched with black thread. She followed me, waving, grinning.

"They won't give me no soda over there, lady," she whined, pointing to the bodega.

I'd seen this one before, and moved away. She turned tricks for drugs between the Dumpster and the candle factory on the side of the service road. She followed me to my building, and I closed the door in her face.

Dozed on couch in blue light. When I was lonely, I sometimes thought of Kai. I still wondered how I could have gotten invited to Paris, what chess piece I should have played. It was the same old shit: I didn't want to go, but I hated being left behind.

He liked to look while he fingered me; he would lie, curled like a fetus, down by my knees, stare into me, then up toward my eyes. In the dark, his face floated, pale and rabid, like a disembodied head.

He hadn't loved me absolutely. He'd saved something for the Frankenstein in his head, made of schoolgirls, hookers, women he hated, strippers, me, and his own cousins.

Once, when he was trashed, he clutched me in a cab: "I'm gonna ride you like a hobbyhorse, you little bitch."

I couldn't stop laughing. I laughed hysterically. "Oh my God," I finally wheezed. "Strike that from the record."

"Why?" he'd slurred petulantly, looking up from where he slumped like an angry child. "Strike what?"

He was eternally a teenager. Loving him kept certain glories alive: fast cars, public sex, stolen liquor, menial labor, cheap cocaine. But that part of him, and of us, eventually began to curdle.

In a Vermont motel room, after celebrating his brother's college graduation, I brushed my teeth, came out to find Kai snoring, cock in hand, muted porn on the TV.

"You retard," I said.

I remember the female star's laziness, glazed eyes, sly smile. It made the guy crazy. I leaned against the headboard, eating mints and deconstructing her style while my boyfriend twitched beside me.

Couldn't sleep.

Was Yves reading in bed, light reflecting yellow off bifocals, teacup steaming next to pajama sleeve? Or was he at Lot 61, cloistered at a table with French and Russian girls, champagne chilling in a dewdropped bucket, arms draped across the backs of their chairs?

Slipped on black kimono. Sipped Dewar's at the kitchen table and scribbled on a pad.

What should I draw? Objects were suspended in my imagination: Kai's gold razor, my mother's white glove, the airplane liquor bottles in my purse, Yves's money clip. Mystical and potent like the candlesticks and cupboards floating down the rabbit hole, and then debris when they clattered to the floor.

Opened the window when I recognized the crying as human. In a doorway alcove of the candle factory, the stitched forehead. Denim jacket, rocking herself. Glass glittering around black sneakers.

"Stop it," I yelled, my voice echoing in the night.

I once heard a kitten wailing under a sidewalk grate, and a crowd gathered to stare down at her marmalade face, but there was no way to get her out.

In the morning, I threw on jeans and trench coat, fake Chanel hoop earrings. Walked a few blocks to Phoebe's Café and had lox on a bagel and cappuccino. At the thrift store across the street, a cat snaked under hemlines, set gowns swaying. I tried on a pink coat that said Scarsdale wife, that said box seats at the ballet, orchid club, deviled eggs, black Mercedes. Her heart must have been settled, made tight as a hotel bed, unlike mine.

I bought red leather gloves on which I could smell the snow of many winters, and a white clutch with gold butterfly clasp. I'd spent almost everything again and couldn't pay October's rent, so balancing the old checkbook no longer mattered.

At this point, I loathed my own company so much I took the L to Union Square just to avoid the solitude of my apartment. I wandered through the cool, purple-lit market that was closing. I inhaled the green perfume of zinnias and thyme as they were reloaded into trucks. Steam rising from a cauldron of cider reminded me of fairy tales. A man withdrew wheels of cheese from a glass case, wrapped them in wax paper.

Maybe I could bum a ride to his farm, where goats kicked like toys in fields. Where magenta leaves crowded thorny branches that drooped with late blackberries. Where someone dragged that morning's trout through flour, laid it in a hot buttered skillet. I knew this Never Land must exist.

On the way home I called Belinda from a pay phone, so she wouldn't see my number, but hung up after one ring. My heart was beating hard. What was wrong with me? It was like making the first call to some boy I loved.

That night, I sat in my orange butterfly chair as if thrown there, unable to get up. It's amazing how a certain time in your life can seem to be a prelude, but when you look back, you realize it was a whole work, with a beginning, middle, and end. Belinda and I got off to a shy start, trying to guess how our agendas differed. The way new friends do. Quickly we discovered we had the same plan: to have no plan. She offered the blank slate I wanted after moving from the Cape.

Such lazy scavenger hunts. Wandering around Chinatown, trying on turquoise silk jackets, beaded sandals. Rubbing rice paper between fingertips. Holding up black-and-gold chopsticks, clicking them once in the air. We'd end up at a Malaysian place, eating roti telur and coconut rice, drunk on tea, a rain of trinkets and china and figurines falling in my mind. Putting days together was like designing a painting: a Hitchcock movie at the Sunshine one snowy afternoon, then steaming pierogis in Greenpoint. Or junk jewelry shops on Thirtieth and Broadway, then fried pork chops at a Spanish restaurant near Delancey, sipping Él Presidentes and looking through our fake gold.

The things we wore were talismans. Sometimes she swiped a gift from a shoot, and I cherished the Vivienne Westwood corset not because it was valuable but because it had been procured subversively, and with a twisted version of generosity. We treated certain clothes as uniforms and, by never taking them off, defined our private eras. Belinda's gray sharkskin jacket was safety-pinned along every seam because she wore it even to sleep. My Costume Nationale boots with the witchy toes were resoled four times. We sometimes rode the train to the Hartford Goodwill, reading the paper on the way, savoring coffee and cheese danishes. The journey was more urgent than the red Jackie O suit one of us might bring home.

Some nights, we spent hours trying on pearls, alligator stilettos, hats, until we looked at the time and realized it was too late to go anywhere.

We didn't belong to anyone, although we tried. We spent time at a Southampton share with third-class models Belinda knew. They played badminton in gold bikinis, speaking a pidgin English made of inside jokes, fashion-world lingo, and bits of every language. Such a strange and beautiful tribe. I sat by the pool while they ridiculed an Italian girl for putting birth control pills inside of her; finally she broke down and cried, and then one held her like a baby. They raced around the lawn shooting water pistols. Two hid in the shade, one brushing the other's long black hair. Late one night, I walked into the kitchen, where the dregs of a party had gathered; the Italian was on hands and knees, snorting Special K from a shag carpet, where it had been spilled, with a straw. I was in awe, sometimes in love, and often horrified by them. But I was not one of them, and neither was Belinda.

She tried to push me into the art world. We went to openings, but the artists were just carbon copies of rock stars, circled by groupies drinking bad wine. These people weren't villains, but I didn't have the credentials or confidence to be invulnerable to all the attitude in the air. I could not kiss the ass of the gallery owner, whose aboriginal face tattoos had been done on the Lower East Side and funded by inherited IBM stock; I could not tell her that pubic hairs taped to a drugstore receipt and selling for six grand was a genius installment.

At Spring Studio, many students were mastering lifestyle, not art. Shuffling around in flannels and chain-smoking like Pollock, but not actually putting paint on canvas. Eventually I met a few true nerds. We'd go out for cheap hamburgers, collaboratively draw for hours on napkins like Ernst did with Breton and Magritte, or we'd design an alphabet of Miró-like hieroglyphics. But one night I got chastised in class for eating the pear from a still life, and I never went back. I used to make fun of the philistines who made fun of modern art, but I missed Jeremy and his aluminum stingrays and his orange moons, his loinclothed Tarzan wading through a lake of stars.

Belinda and I, it seemed, were an indestructible pair. Even Kai didn't break up our sisterhood. In fact, we sometimes felt like family. Once, a photographer gave Belinda ballet tickets. She invited David, and the four of us got decked out and took the subway to Lincoln Center. Sitting in that dark red-velvet cavern, seated between friends, spellbound by the chandelier and the jewels in the ballerina's hair and the wet eyes of the dancers and the dim lights in the orchestra pit, I couldn't tell where the love I felt began and where it ended.

Kai and I hosted film nights, renting the *Godfather* series, or a couple Truffaut movies. He made old-fashioned popcorn, pouring melted butter over the bowl, and handed out cold root beers. He and I and Belinda would lounge on big pillows in the flickering light and laugh, cry, throw kernels at the screen.

We took Belinda along on a late-August weekend in Brookhaven. Trevor, the head chef where Kai worked, owned a summer home on a canal where morning glories bloomed in the reeds. We took his boat to the flats near Fire Island, clammed while the American flag snapped in the hot wind and blue from the waves flashed on the hull. Even after Kai and I took a cold shower that evening at the house, the sun was still in me and with me. He and I were shucking clams in the kitchen when first Trevor then, a few minutes later, Belinda emerged from Trevor's bedroom: sheepish, tousled, and beautiful. We sat at the glass table on the porch. The bluefish, under a layer of aioli and fat tomato slices, had been baked in tinfoil. We drank a Pinot Gris from the North Fork. The only light was a candle in a hurricane glass, and our shadows stretched through the screen onto the lawn, almost touching moonlit water.

We did scrape together, over the years, a crew of bandits. Outcasts and reactors. But the freedom of being on the outside faded into habit. Belinda and I went to the same places, but they'd either gotten louder, or the crowd had become younger, or the DJs had gone commercial. The turquoise silk was polyester, and the chopsticks were cheap plastic. We should have changed, but we didn't, or couldn't, or wouldn't. My mother got sick. Then she got sicker. Belinda tried to help, but she didn't understand. So when she tried to talk, I wanted to be alone. When she left me alone, I accused her of being selfish. It's possible I did the same thing to Kai. What I know was that we couldn't find the heart of the city anymore, no matter how hard we looked, when it had at one point been everywhere.

One day, Kai said something about my mother. I'd probably provoked him into agreeing with something I didn't really believe. I stormed out of the apartment and went to Belinda's without calling. She buzzed me in, and I stomped up the stairs. At this point she was seeing Matty, but not exclusively. I found her on her bed, in a dress from the night before, cheap cologne hanging in the air. Her eye makeup was iridescent and greasy. She let me kiss her.

I clomped around the place as if I lived there, high on anger. "Let's just have a drink, B, because this girl needs one. Deserves one."

In the bathroom: red heels kicked off in front of the toilet, a tampon whose end was barely pinked floating in the bowl.

"Hair of the dog, sweetheart," I said when she didn't answer.

Reentering her room, I cocked my head; she hadn't moved, her blond head sunk in the pillow, eyes half open. When I told her she'd make the perfect drawing model and dug my book from my bag, she barely shrugged. But the minute I started sketching her bare feet, she pulled her body up. Standing to look out the window, she struck a match four or five times before it lit.

"I can't do this anymore," she said.

I was silent for a moment. "That's okay. I'm not really feeling artistic anyway."

She exhaled smoke. "That's not what I meant."

I stared at the silhouette left on the blanket. I tried to hide my humiliation.

◇◇◇◇◇

Eventually I got out of the orange chair and into bed. The next morning I broke down and called Yves, but he didn't answer. I couldn't spend another night alone, so I pleaded with Chico to come to Brooklyn. Plan Eat Thai was packed with people smoking, laughing, shoveling noodles, slamming sake.

We left the hibachi table with clothes smelling of meat smoke. At Blondie's, a coke spot on the edge of the Northside, we bought a blue bag in an old telephone closet. In the back room, we did lines at a card table. The bartender in the main room, a Latina girl with braces, wore a black spandex skirt that didn't conceal the bottom inches of her stockings' control top. She served us beers.

"I liked Kelly," Chico insisted, pulling a white pebble from his nostril hair. "He made a good Manhattan."

"He rubbed me the wrong way."

"You didn't like how private he was, Lee. That's what it was. You couldn't get him drunk."

"No," I said crisply. "I didn't like that I was forced to give him a job."

"Then why did you?"

I picked at the beer label. "Because I had to."

"No you didn't."

I sighed. "You know what I mean."

"Lee, you can do anything you want. You just take the easy way out every time."

"That's kind of harsh," I spat out.

I begged to stay, but Chico eventually said we had to leave.

"Lee, I've got things to do tomorrow," he said.

"Then why did you come out at all?" I asked irrationally.

"To be honest, to keep you company, girl, and this is the thanks I get."

Even though the sun was rising, it pissed me off so much that we were leaving that I stopped talking to him. Before we stumbled out, thugs checked the street since it was past legal closing time. A glossy Town Car waited in the empty landscape. Chico slumped in the backseat. The horizon was creamy orange and blue, though the sky was still dark and starry.

Chico said good night and tried to kiss my cheek when we pulled up to my house, but I pulled away and said nothing. I slunk up the stairs dragging my purse, *clunk clunk clunk*, on each step. I wanted to wake the whole building. Even my heart was pale.

I made it to work in a white safari jacket and white jeans picked off my floor. Josh laughed when I wouldn't take off the black sunglasses, and I gave him the finger. Poison moved sluggishly through my veins.

The lunch special was cassoulet. All I could get down, though, was half a mayonnaise sandwich. The perfume of dying leaves and blue air was carried in on coats, hair, slacks. I called Yves again, and he answered.

"Oh, thank God," I said.

"Thank God for what?" he asked, but I could tell he was smiling.

"Will you hang out with me tonight?" I pleaded. "I'll plan a night. I'll be proactive and caring."

He laughed, but acquiesced. "You're unbalanced, Lee."

"I know, I know, I know."

When I got home, I decided I should be striking. But the nausea, if anything, was increasing. So I mixed a drink and cut lines.

I sprayed Jicky behind ears and between legs. Pulled on a vintage black dress with cap sleeves and belt. Very Sophia Loren. A shimmer of blue on eyelids, red lipstick. My Helmut Lang heels with leather ankle ties. I rocked out in the mirror to Run-DMC. Imagined I was in a documentary of my own life.

In the beginning, knowing I'd never match his generosity, I brought gifts to Yves's house for fun. I'd arrive with a peony between my teeth, or a string-tied box of eclairs from the Mafia café in Williamsburg. He so loved the creamed herring I got him from Russ & Daughters that he was caught eating from the plastic container, which was, in Yves's world, a sin. More than anything, I wanted to give him something tonight, but I couldn't think of what, and I feared anything I got would look inconsequential, silly. Somehow I'd left behind the place where my whims meant something to us.

After Yves and I kissed and hugged, we squeezed each other's hands: secret apology, silent forgiveness. The fireplace at Boughalem was roaring, so I took off my white leather jacket. The hostess, her bob so lustrous it was blue, brought me a Johnnie Walker.

He was relaxed, and talked about some art opening incident that involved a ferret. I chain-smoked, half listening. Once in a while, pouting, I sneaked a glance at my heart-shaped face in the window. I visited the ladies' room. When escargot arrived, I couldn't eat. I smoked, watched him fork meat from the broth.

"I don't want to eat them all, love," he said. "Share."

"I saw a documentary on snails, darling, and I just can't," I lied.

He apologized, continued eating and telling his story. I put on lipstick in the reflection of a spoon. Let a smile play over my lips as though everything in the world were innocent and pleasing.

◇◇◇◇◇

At the movie I was scattered, my mind chattering, but ever since I was young I'd had a crush on Marilyn Monroe, and she always enchanted me, coaxed me away from the world. Watching the satin gloves crease on her plump arm, the diamond wink on her white neck, I wondered why no one saved her. The million-dollar question. She threw herself to the public, rained down like wedding rice till there was nothing left. She gave away the part that isn't for giving. But I guess that's how God created her: a spy's instructions to be burned once they're read.

It was about a week later when I got the unexpected call.

I sat on a stool at the far end of the dim and dirty Mars Bar. Strange meeting place. A Rubenesque girl on my left with blond pageboy and tongue ring smoked Capris; exhaling, she narrowed heavily lined eyes at me. I held two pointer fingers at her in the sign of the cross. She looked away.

"Lee," he said behind me, and I jumped.

My coat lay over the stool on my right. He pointed, asked if he could sit there. "Long as you don't fart on it," I said, crushing my cigarette and lighting another.

What the hell did I just say?

Kelly stared at the bartender, a platinum-blond man with a dimpled chin and black stubble. Kelly seemed not so much thirsty as unable to look at me.

"Totally didn't expect to hear from you," I said.

Big shoulders hunched forward in a button-down so thin his tattoos showed through the pale fabric. Hair dark at roots. Pink sheen on cheekbones. He darted a look at me, coughed. Spoke a whole sentence that couldn't be heard over loud Ramones. I cupped a hand around my ear, motioned for a do-over.

"We got off on the wrong foot." He took a sip of beer, foam

mustaching his upper lip. "I was hoping to clear the air. I don't like burned bridges."

I looked into my scotch, stirred the oily drink.

"You going to sue me for your job back or something?"

He shook his head vehemently, like a child, tendrils of hair flapping. "I want to apologize. I was a jackass. I'm going through some weird stuff at the moment."

Wet brown eyes. Mottled cheeks. Uh-oh, was he about to cry? No. Sneeze.

"God bless you," I said.

"Allergies," he said, blowing his nose in a cocktail napkin.

"You *were* a jackass," I mused, scanning the graffiti on the walls.

Kelly looked at me, alarmed.

"So was I," I said quickly. "Yves almost killed me when I told him you were fired."

He nodded, as though I'd said something profound, then clapped hands on big thighs. "Well," he said, "I gotta run. I'm glad we did this. I mean, thanks for meeting me."

"That's it?"

He looked me in the eye. "Yeah. That's it."

As he stood, I told him to come back to work the day after tomorrow, to be there at four.

I realized he was about to hit me. I'd fired this man. I braced myself; he towered above me, the dark face, the fists clenched. He leaned down and kissed me, his mouth hot on mine. His hand gripped my jaw as if he could turn me somehow toward him more, closer to him, but the intensity of his mouth didn't change. He just yearned, a feeling I tasted: beer, blood, a dark red love that blossomed petal after petal after petal into my own mouth.

As he hurried to the door, he stubbed his toe on a stool. "Shit," he hissed, tucked his hair. He didn't look back.

⟡⟡⟡

I lay in bed that night like an angel, a baby bundled in white cloth, a kitten wrapped in a white cardigan. The scuttle of roaches, flies tapping against the window, the highway thunder: nothing bothered me. Nothing. I lay bathed in cold gold light and felt that hand gripping me, felt it grip my jaw over and over again as if it were the hand of God taking me like his daughter and breathing life into my throat, touching my lips with possibility. I just lay there on fire, not a raging fire that would turn me to ashes, but a fire that started as one lavender flame between my legs and traveled along a line of gasoline straight to my heart.

I walked up my street under an autumn sun that was white in the center, white around the edges. Passed the one-eyed pug whose empty eye was a flower of black leather. He slept in that shade every day. A trail of ants ran up his saucer; I'd seen an old lady reach from the basement unit window to fill the dish with sugar and milk. I felt him watching as I walked away, and I heard, from a window high above the yellow leaves, someone waking up to Al Green.

I was remembering my fat friend Stuart, curly headed like a cherub, almost forgotten forever until today. When we were ten, we'd wander into the woods and lie on top of each other. My God, I remembered the musk of dirt, the bugs crawling on our skin, the perfume of lilies of the valley. Hands sticky with pollen and chocolate, and all I had to do was kiss his cheek and I would come. But what did that mean? There were no sexual parts yet. Only an afternoon lush with heat and body and heart and breath and pleasure and dirt and blossom, coming through us in rushes of love.

On the way back from the store that evening, I paused to shift the paper bag to my other hip. It was an Indian summer night, and I was sweating in my coat. Buildings loomed red or avocado green in streetlamp lights. A dog snorted through an overturned garbage pail. On the corner of North Fifth and Driggs, a garden was enclosed by a chain-link fence: a small, glossy darkness. Here and there, the pale smudge of flower. And occupying the square, dozens of fireflies. I put my groceries down, pressed my face to the fence, clung to the wire. I watched them loop around one another, golden abdomens flushing with light.

When Kelly walked into work, my hands started shaking with stage fright. He wore blue jeans, white button-down, yellow necktie hand-painted with roses. Wet hair combed back into elastic. Wide, easy smile.

"Hey, jackass," I greeted him, and looked at his tie since I couldn't look at his face. "Find that thing in a Dumpster?"

He froze, then picked up his tie, pondered it. "No, at the Salvation—"

"Better step on it," I said in a strangely paternal voice. "Don't make me doubt my decision."

I regretted each and every word *as* it came out of my mouth. Down in the office, I chain-smoked till the room was opaque. Pulled red hair across my face.

"I'm a loser," I said over and over in a surprised voice, as if it were a discovery. "I'm a loser. I. Am. A. Loser."

Kelly and I spent the week like butterflies, jerking around each other. Every time I saw him, I became embarrassed. I said stupid things. He'd throw the dish towel over his shoulder and smile. He seemed intent on waiting it out.

One day, he asked if I was, in fact, painting.

"There are paintings in my head," I said, unable to lie. "But if I manage to start them, the ideas will be ruined."

He laughed, buffing champagne glasses. "Can you talk about them, or is it secret?"

"They're about nothing," I said, warming up to the topic.

"I don't follow."

"Nothing is the only expertise I've gained in a number of years, you see. So I want to show nothing."

"So you want to make something out of nothing," he conceded, shelving the glasses.

"But that would negate the whole statement," I reminded him. "So I'm at a crossroads. Nihilism is a bitch."

Walked down to the office, hit my palm against my forehead.

At closing that night, I was counting money at the bar when someone knocked on the locked door. Yves had been out on the town. Refracted through moonlit glass, he looked like a hologram.

"I brought you something from the party," he said when let in, and held out a Louis Vuitton shopping bag. I made a fuss over the gift so I didn't have to kiss him in front of Kelly.

"Yves, I take it," Kelly said, extended his hand, and they shook. "I get to thank you in person for helping me out."

"My pleasure," Yves said in his golden voice.

Everyone waited for them to continue speaking, but they said nothing else. I grabbed my cigarettes and forced a yawn, indicated that I wanted to leave. I wasn't uncomfortable: no one suspected anyone of anything. I was overjoyed. It had just occurred to me that I could have both.

◇◇◇◇◇

In Yves's bed, we went at it kind of hard—hard for us, at least. I called in my pool boys, lawn boys, vacuum-cleaner salesmen. My blue-collar angels with no faces. Who knows what Yves recruited. We were alienated from each other, as if lace separated our bodies: we could feel the other's warmth but not the skin. I was safe with him, and safe from him.

When he returned to bed from lengthy ablutions, I asked for a bedtime story.

His words glistened like icicles in the dark.

He told me about a fire in his childhood town. The favorite bistro was burning down. He told the story slowly, sparely, taking time to describe flaming curtains flanking a view of cold blue river, but using few words. Before the fire trucks arrived, he and his friend jumped through the falling rafters to the courtyard. Back there the trellises crackled and fell, the burning skeletons of dahlias tumbling to brick.

My head lay on his chest, his heart warming my ear.

Yves and his friend knew the fountain pond was full of coins, and they scooped centimes out of the boiling water with their hands.

"Did you get out okay?" I whispered.

"What a silly question," he said. "I'm here, aren't I?"

FOUR

◇◇◇◇◇

I drank at every vine.
    The last was like the first.
I came upon no wine
    So wonderful as thirst.

—EDNA ST. VINCENT MILLAY, from "Feast"

The estrangement I'd loved the night before crept into the morning and alienated me from myself. In Yves's bathroom, my reflection was a half-finished acrylic portrait by an amateur.

The composition was creepy. Black nail polish picked up black tile, toothpaste in the sink echoed the turquoise burning under the skin of my eye sockets. Negligee askew, the wrinkles unnatural, crooked. Shoulders greasy as hard-boiled egg. Even my roan hair gleamed redder, ruder, cheaper.

The features didn't come together to make a face. The clues didn't combine to tell a story. Mascara-blurred eyes seemed sad, but why? The planes didn't create a plausible room: dimensions were off, perspective impossible. An unconvincing document, as works of art go.

That night, Camilla was throwing Sam a birthday party. I knew Camilla from high school. They knew each other from Brown. A painter and a photo rep: I didn't like either of them. Their loft, in the converted McKibbin Street factory, was a diorama of bohemian life: orange Vespa, candles melting on the floor, paintbrushes in kitchen sink. I wore a trench coat and jeans, pearl earrings, cat eyes; I was on a terrible mission, and I didn't know it.

Camilla's sister, Sloane, opened wine while Camilla arranged Stilton, black grapes. Ribbed, snowy neck, fine wrists, and cheeks ripe as cherries. Sloane, who was a filmmaker, also lived here in Bushwick, a helicopter searchlighting the streets even at that moment, but she and Camilla both could have been Westport wives.

Sam rolled a joint at a paint-scabbed worktable. Behind him

on the easel, his wife's portrait of him: sand, pale body in black briefs, gray tide sliding onto canvas. In the painting, Sam's curly black hair obscured his profile as he bent to examine the legs of the dead horseshoe crab he held by the tail.

In life, now, he hunched in the opposite direction, licking the paper to seal it. The tension between him and his image would make a good photograph, and he knew it, and that was the essence of his art-world life: one successful juxtaposition after another.

I stared at a guy in a Sex Pistols T-shirt and a girl in a gypsy dress, dark hair on her arms like a sensual moss. They didn't belong at this party. They kissed in front of the factory windows. Their bodies reflected in the lavender panes: a triptych of valentines.

These two probably made out every morning regardless of dragon breath, hangover, or the stranger sleeping on the air mattress next to them. They got fired over and over from shitty jobs. Lived on peanut butter sandwiches, planned road trips that would never happen, and watched cult movies while roommates ranted on the phone to the landlord. Pissed without shutting the bathroom door. They were playmates. They got their hands dirty. All the stories they told each other were true.

A blond boy sucked the spliff, then coughed and continued hacking, blindly holding it out to the crowd. I took a long drag, held it, blew a cloud. Passed it nonchalantly.

Immediately, I went deaf. My skin broke out in sweat, and I felt it turn white. I played with the charm on my bracelet as though it was a toy. The blond boy was splayed on the couch like a tuberculosis patient taking in the sun.

I drifted away to gaze through the glass. The purple tint deepened the heartbroken landscape. In the junkyard, the white Sunnydale milk truck tilted like a shipwreck. Next to it, a dirt backyard. On the porch, a dog threw itself against the restraint of its chain, barking up at us.

When I recovered enough composure, I poured whiskey into a cup. I took my third piece of cake to the couch. Looked left then right, and unbuttoned the top of my jeans.

Took a fresh whiskey with me to the record player. Lifted the needle midsong.

"I put that on." The blond kid pouted. "It was my favorite."

I handed it to him so he could put it back into the jacket. I smiled in a way I hoped would comfort him, and winked. "I think you were alone, there, sailor. You're putting us all to sleep."

Two men stood under the turquoise lantern, the glowing paper painted with orange flowers on black branches. Hands in pockets, the strangers looked Germanic and severe, with boldly sculpted faces, sunken eyes.

I walked up, beaming, hands on hips. "My name is Lee," I said brightly. "Flirt with me."

I don't know what I was in the middle of telling them, but I vaguely sensed one of them gesturing to someone. Their friend joined us. I introduced myself to him. Then, with theatrical reluctance, he said they all really had to get going.

"Oh, that's too bad," I said.

The other two agreed, waving good-bye to me as if I were a child, and they moved to the other side of the room.

The blond boy's eyes were glazed blue slits. I kicked his foot. "Come with me."

He opened his eyes a millimeter.

"Did you kick me?" he asked.

"No," I said.

On the street, an Isuzu truck was burned out, its charred doors open like wings.

"I don't like coke," he whined.

"Shut up," I said, and held my key under his nostril.

Laughter from the window upstairs fell down through darkness, and a couple straggled out through the stairwell, a piece of cake on a paper plate in his hands, a ratty fur thrown around her bare shoulders. She stopped and swayed, pressing powder to her chin in a mirror while he watched.

I kissed the blond boy with my eyes open.

I stumbled up a few flights. Knocked where I heard music. A man opened the door. His black hair was spiked, eyes lined in electric blue. He asked if the music was too loud.

"No, no," I mumbled. "Came to get my coat."

"Came to get your coat," he repeated doubtfully.

"I'm leaving," I explained, working to form words. "I gotta get my coat."

At this, he smiled, with his mouth at least, not his eyes. "Come on in and get your coat, then, honey."

After the door closed and I was standing in the middle of the loft, it finally hit me I was in the wrong apartment.

A cheap standing lamp did little, and most of the space lay in shadow. Inside the gold circle, two white kids slumped on a tartan couch, sneakers propped on a coffee table littered with smoldering ashtrays, tinfoil, soda cans.

"Sit down," the man said. "I insist," he said, when I started to object.

A short-haired dog kept nuzzling my crotch, and the man watched me push him away.

"He likes you," he said.

No one spoke. So I looked around the loft. Two kids were sleeping on a pink mattress. In the corner, a gaunt black girl played Atari, but she seemed not to be connecting the movements her hands made on the joystick to the Pac-Man in the maze.

"I have a question," I said to the host.

I'd tried heroin many times, but only in dreams. My sleeping mind would send me drifting like a doll through hallways, along highways, on what I just knew was an accurate ride. My soul was somehow acquainted with that high, as if it were my own sea level, an equilibrium to achieve.

"What are you guys doing?" I asked meaningfully.

I asked, knowing that with this substance, for some reason, the game would be forfeited. I would never get to fall in love. I would never learn to belong to the world. I might live for many years, of course, but it would be the end of me.

He narrowed red eyes, then examined his blue fingernails, flaking off some polish.

"Would you share?" I said.

He looked up, scanned my body as if he might want to have sex with me, even though I knew he didn't.

"I think you're lost, darling," he said.

They all looked. Finally the man jerked his thumb at the door.

"Best way out is the way you came in," he said.

Then I walked, coatless, down Bushwick Avenue. Tears. Streaks of mascara down my cheeks. Stopped at a bodega for a forty of Olde English, and the man who bagged my bottle actually asked if I was okay. "Chu okay, huhn-ney?" I passed packs of men in do-rags, slumped on bikes or assembled around the open doors of vans, Jay-Z and OutKast cranked up. None of them leered. They were afraid of me, in a way. "Oh, shit," they murmured, and gave me room to pass.

I chugged the beer, threw the bottle down an empty street, cherished its smash on asphalt. Stopped at the deli next to my place, bought a big white Entenmann's cake and another forty, and perched on my stoop.

At four in the morning, I somehow made it to Black Betty. Picked up a kid from Tijuana. He lived in a honeycomb of rooms, his bed separated from the next by a Bart Simpson beach towel hung from the ceiling. Prep-cook uniform, soiled, by the door.

"You're all fucked up, little girl," he said, watching me tangle my shirt around my neck. He pinched my nipple without real interest. When I offered to buy a condom at the bodega, he let me go alone. He knew I wouldn't be back.

Woke up in my own bed, pillowcase wet with puke that smelled of malt liquor and coconut icing.

The B.Q.E. exit outside my building was the last before the bridge to Manhattan. All evening, I sat by my window. Dully, I watched pairs of cars pull onto the service road like mating dragonflies. Dealer in front, buyer in back.

That night, I went to the Laundromat and watched TV while my clothes sloshed in circles. On *COPS*, police chased a woman with a yellow mullet through construction, and she scrambled under a half-built house like a hunted dog. She started digging into red mud between pillars. The cameraman followed, the film jiggling, belt buckle scraping earth. When they caught up, her hands were bloodied, white shorts filthy.

"Are you on something, ma'am?" they drawled over and over.

I could have been an episode last night, I thought. Redhead in a bodega, eyeliner drawn down into Harlequin daggers, looking at white cake. Swaying, she picked it up, dropped it, frosting stuck to the cellophane window.

I'd always believed an innocent attitude made events innocent. I'd survived debaucheries, and afterward even felt that the girl in her white Sunday dress inside me had been renewed, forged in the fire one more time. I now doubted that mechanism. I now doubted myself. Innocence was finite and could not be regenerated. Like spinal fluid. I knew this because I had run out.

Taking reservations on the phone, I avoided Kelly's gaze. Tapping the pen on the book, I cringed, wondering what he saw when he looked at me.

When I was little, I'd had so many ambitions. I saw them lined up like Barbies in boxes, accessories rubber-banded to their plastic wrists. Lee the fireman. Lee the trapeze artist. Lee the ballerina. When I really thought about it, though, I'd never planned on being anything, which is natural, I guess, for a child. I'd dreamed of being this or that, but never thought through to becoming anything. My first dream was to be a nurse, but that had to do with a hat no one wore anymore. And now my dream of being a painter was looking just as juvenile.

Kelly ate an apple, reading a newspaper, standing as he always did as if lunging into while pushing away from the bar. He grinned at me, and I smiled meekly at the apple.

Painting had been the only way to crystallize, distill, and

change ordinary life. It had been alchemy. But at some point I'd lost the trick. I'd taken such bad care of myself that I was no longer talented. I had a feeling it was gone forever.

So many land mines in this new territory called adulthood. Talent has a window. Freedom sometimes becomes a trap. We may die before we finish our dreams. Actually, that we die is a pretty big surprise by itself. We can't spend innocence without accounting. Relationships are contracts. We partner not just for love but because we become too weak to make it alone.

My junior year in boarding school I made the first big mistake of my life. Her name was Lucy.

She was a townie, but not an ordinary one. Her father, a film producer, rarely visited their Massachusetts home, let her live there with his ex-girlfriends or his assistants or no one. She drove a black BMW. Her skin was so bad it sometimes bled. Her body was stocky, white as potato flesh. Everyone hated her. So I became her best friend.

She introduced me to the particular liberty sometimes found in motel rooms. Despite dirty bedspreads and smoky curtains, a room could still offer anonymity. A tabula rasa for the poetry of amphetamines or grain alcohol. I liked not coming face to face with a childhood toy while tripping. I liked a place where nothing could remind me of myself if I made sure to avoid the mirror. And my phantoms to this day are probably curled up in those motor lodges, smoking, watching game shows, and coming down or coming to.

One night, we wanted coke, but the regular guy wasn't responding. So we went to meet a man and his wife who were eating burgers at Friendly's. In the car on the way back to the motel, she told me they didn't have what we'd wanted, but she'd gotten something else.

Sitting cross-legged on a mauve bedspread in room 201, we smoked crack off a Dr Pepper can. I succumbed immediately to a chemical hurricane. When I came back, she was on round two. I didn't want any more, but she urged me to try again. After that, I couldn't take it. All I wanted was to watch television, but she turned out the lights, told me to be quiet. I sat in the dark, listened as she sucked the soda can and fell back, moaning.

She didn't want to have fun. She did it all to mark herself, like carving a bedpost with sexual touchdowns. I preferred fun, but I also understood her motives. When I was a kid, I had shaved one forearm in the bath. At school the next day, the hairless skin filled me with dread. But it was exhilarating, too, that in what seemed an accidental world, I had forced change. When Lucy and I finished a Rumplemintz bottle, Led Zeppelin on the alarm clock radio, Bible as a coaster, we were queens of disaster.

I'd cut Lucy loose by senior year, convinced she was dark and I was light. I sneered at her walking through snow in wet black Converse high-tops with a new nose ring and a freshman. Started a rumor that she was a lesbian. Even claimed I'd seen her cut a cat open in the garage of an abandoned house, sacrificing its blood for Satan. I did all this to make a distinction that didn't exist.

Got up in the middle of the night, manic, dead set. I'd had a vision. Pulled out a box of oil sticks and a pad from under the bed. The names on the giant crayons thrilled me as much as they first had in high school: alizarin crimson, burnt sienna, raw umber. They formed the periodic table of my ideas. I rushed an underpainting using my fingertips. The oil was slick, grimy, and I loved it. From tenth grade on, I'd been loyal to oils: they were the only medium in which I could create light.

Sitting at the kitchen table in boxers and a wife-beater, I tried to re-create that lantern at Camilla's loft, its luminous blue, those glowing orange flowers. I saw it hanging in a void. Swinging in blackness. I worked.

Within an hour, I came to my senses, stared at the page. I was waking from a good dream, forced to realize it had only been a dream. It was paper and paint. I felt elated that I'd failed, that I'd been right in fearing that I would fail, and defeated, and foolish.

Sat there for a while, absorbed the strange euphoria and disappointment like a snake moving a rat through its body. At the sink, I eventually lit the corner of the paper with a Bic. Only way to make that lantern burn.

After dinner a few nights later, I peeked into Yves's study. He was drinking Perrier and smoking, brown cigarettes crumpled into ashtray. Phone pressed to chin by shoulder, hands typing on laptop.

I tossed salts into the tub, feeling shitty and sorry for myself. I sat on the edge and gazed at tile until it was obscured by steam. Took off clothes, left them in a pile. Gasped when I stepped in, then lounged, skin red below water and pale above.

I heard the thud, but it was the subsequent groan that made me sit up, wild-eyed.

I stepped out, threw on silk robe, ran into hall trying to belt it. Yves had made it to the office threshold. He sat on the floor like a boy playing with toys, but his shoulders slumped and his eyes saw nothing. I took his face in my hands.

"Yves!" I shouted. I shook his face.

I punched his shoulder, and he flinched in slow motion but his face didn't change. "Come on," I said, even louder.

Then I called 911. "He's dead."

"Feel his wrist. Pick up his wrist."

I held his wrist, but he didn't lift his eyes.

"Oh my God he's so dead!" I cried.

"Do you feel a pulse?" she asked severely.

"Don't yell at me!" I answered.

"Lee," Yves said thickly.

"He said my name!" I told the woman.

"Yves, Yves," I said, kissing him. "You said my name."

He was standing before the EMT guys arrived. He was collected enough to send me away when they buzzed. His primary emotion seemed to be shame. As the group conversed in gentle and formal voices, I looked into the bathroom mirror. My heart had become silent. The robe, blue with flamingos on it, was soaked to the skin like a tattoo. I realized I'd been waiting for this, not willing it, not dreading it. An autonomous part of me had been collecting premonitions and clues.

"Is there someone here?" I heard a man say. "Someone who can come with us?"

"No," Yves said gruffly. "No, I'm alone now."

His window looked at the East River, spires and smokestacks seamed with beige light to the sky. Headlights and taillights on the bridges. I sat, McDonald's bag on the floor, and watched him breathe. Picked cheeseburger-bun crumbs from my fur lapel and ate them.

Since I first saw him collapsed in his office, I'd gone through about eighteen moods. I'd forgotten that just one moment, one phone call, can catapult you into a new dimension. In a cab to the hospital, I'd relived a jagged anger at the threat of losing someone. Pissed and defensive as if someone were fucking with me on purpose. When the doctor turned me out of the room for a spell, I'd walked outside for an hour, hating everyone. This rage turned into self-pity, a gross and milky film of depression. I'd stood on a corner, let the DON'T WALK turn to WALK then to DON'T WALK then to WALK, unable to cross the street. Then I'd had that stage-set feeling. (When my mother died, I realized she had to be somewhere else. I'd never thought of this world as a place, because it was the only place. If she was elsewhere, though, this was somewhere. That had suddenly made the universe look like a rickety theater.) But coming back and seeing him awake, if unsettled, had ignited a strange calm. I was giddy, even. The world had conspired to make us both vulnerable at the same time. We matched, for once.

Burped quietly, took off stilettos, and lay on the bed with my coat over me, spooning him.

He was gaunt, eye sockets lilac and deepened. Coming off him was a pungent sweat. His spirit was wet, like a newborn. I rubbed my uncovered feet together, thinking the red polish could use a touch-up.

"Did you see a white light?" I whispered.

"What?" he said roughly.

"Did they try to make you stay?"

"Oh, Christ, Lee. You watch too many movies."

Even though I had the night off, Yves sent me home. But my heart wouldn't leave him. So I sat at my kitchen table with the pad. Oil pastels, their tips flat and grainy, labels tattered, arrayed in front of me. I twisted off the beer cap, tossed it across the room into the sink. Lit a smoke and leaned back.

When I'd said good-bye, Yves had nodded weakly, his yellow-white hair wild as Mozart's. It was hard to keep a straight face. He reminded me of a beautiful woman who'd had a nervous breakdown.

A vision from childhood came to me. At a beach club, I'd faced off with a swan that was twice my height, hissing, opening his white wings yellowed with pollution. Adults circled us, calling me away, but I'd been paralyzed by fear and awe and absurdity. The bird was frightening because he was threatened, and threatening because he was frightened. But what I couldn't get over was that he had legs. Swans were always gliding over the water; my young mind had believed their undersides were smooth hulls of white feathers.

Now I saw a diptych. The first painting: a plane of sand, the swan, the white child, the sun-bleached cabanas in the background. The second: a bed, a white-haired man, his pale face. Both pictures would be like fields of snow. The only colors would be vanilla, ivory, ocher, periwinkle.

Nowadays, when images conspired in my head, they exploded, like stars, and turned to dust. The event was always over before the painting began. But the power of this fusion lasted as I sketched. I worked for a couple hours, but was afraid to press my luck, and stopped. It felt like a fluke. I couldn't move to canvas.

Standing on Houston's meridian near Sixth, I noticed a tree's red berries, elongated like pearl drops, wet with sunshine. Saw pumpkins in shop windows. In Minetta Park, a lone azalea blossom stood up in the copper-leafed bush. A calm dragged behind me like a wake.

He'd had an EKG, and they booked him for an overnight at the Mayo Clinic in December. But basically they couldn't say for sure if it had been nothing at all, or a minor stroke, or something more serious. Now he opened his door to me in a black V-neck sweater, hair wet and combed, face icy and vigorous again. I flushed with pleasure at seeing him look strong. Holding my hand, he sauntered through the living room. He looked me in the eye, said conspiratorially: "Hope you're hungry."

A table was set in the middle of the room. A low and fat white bouquet of lilies, gardenias, camellias, orchids, roses. Plates were arranged with death-row decadence. Kumamoto oysters with mignonette sauce, the vinegar crammed with minced shallots. Oily caviar piled in a glass dish, on crushed ice in a silver bowl. Warmed blini with crème fraîche. Dom, with its bat-wing label, tilted in the bucket.

"I'm sure as hell hungry now, daddy."

Greasy-haired Jean-Marc, a Raoul's busboy, stood with a serving napkin over one arm. He sneered, he couldn't help it, the chocolate fleck of a mole stretching on his upper lip.

My heart was slow, open, as if sexually languid. I remembered how it felt to sit with Yves in the beginning, not wanting to be anywhere else. While Jean-Marc refilled my champagne, I asked if the doctor had prescribed anything. Yves accused me of wanting his pills.

"You don't need to be suspicious all the time," I said. "Maybe I just want to look after you a little bit."

"No, no," he said. "Not necessary."

"But it would be fun to play nurse."

He looked at me with intensity. "I take care of you, Lee."

"You do," I agreed uncertainly.

"I'd like to take better care of you."

"Yves, what's wrong?"

I thought he was angry by the way he wiped his mouth with the napkin. I thought he'd dropped something under the table when he started to go down on one knee.

In a Dior box lined with mink, the unusual ring was four-petal sapphire flowers embedded in a tall band of tiny diamonds.

"I want you to have everything. You can move in here, or we can get a new place. You can work with a designer, build out a loft from scratch. The way you live, child. It's beneath you."

I laughed because it was all I could do. "What do you mean?"

He made a face, as if this was a delicate topic. Then he shrugged. "You live next to a highway. You wear secondhand clothes, some dead person's things."

"It's called *vintage*."

"In any case, you know what I'm talking about."

I swallowed a glass of champagne, poured a new one. It was strange to be looking down at him. It was strange, in fact, to be alive.

"Maybe," I said, burping through my nose.

"What's that, love?"

"Maybe is my answer tonight."

After he stood, he tried to give me the ring to keep while I decided, but I vehemently pushed it away.

"Do not trust me with that, baby," I said. "If I'm not wearing it, I'll lose it."

He grinned wolfishly, tucked a napkin into his collar as Jean-Marc served scarlet lobsters. I watched him eat, almost unable to eat myself, shocked and overjoyed and tripping. The blue and white gems smoldered in the box. Every clump of pollen on the lily, every gradation of orange on the lobster was acutely meaningful. The room was saturated with meaning. I'd always known Yves wanted me, the way he wanted any luxury. I never believed one day he might need me.

"Take your time, Lee. I'll give you however much time you need."

My eyes teared. "Thank you."

He glanced up, smiled again, cracked a claw.

✧✧✧✧✧

Four o'clock, lunch shift over, dinner not begun, and it was already darkening. Outside, movie lights glared on a camera crew surrounding a checkered cab. Trailers lined the block. Kelly and I drank sherry at the bar, watching, awkward as teenagers.

He was pale and needed to shave.

"You okay?" I asked.

"Ahgg," he groaned, running hands through hair. "Weird morning, is all. Well, bad morning. I was on a subway that hit someone."

I made a face. "That's awful."

"It was. It was awful."

"Did you see the person?"

"Uh, no. Just saw all the cops. They wouldn't let us out; they wouldn't open the doors. But we felt it, the train running over something. Word came through the cars."

I could feel my eyes shining with morbid light. "Girl or boy?"

He rubbed his stubbled jaw. Then he looked at me. "I don't know."

"Young or old?"

He looked at me an extra minute. "Don't know."

Under electric moonlight, a woman got into the cab, and out of it, then into it again. Kelly was staring as if about to ask me something. So I got up, blurted that I had to pee, and hurried downstairs.

Listening to Yves breathe in the dark, I imagined myself in a white Yves Saint Laurent suit, with a wide hat and cane, like

Bianca Jagger. "Sweet Thing" by Van Morrison playing as I strolled down the aisle. I imagined drinking from a champagne bottle, slumped on a hotel room toilet. Yves and I poised in front of red curtains, pushing white cake into each other's mouth, bulb flashing. If I could make sense of the wedding, I might comprehend marriage. But it was too medieval: powder-blue garter, veil, first waltz, bloody sheet.

My mother told me love was work. I don't know if she believed or practiced that, but she loved to say it. I wanted desperately to take that leap because something had to change, because a window of chance had opened, because I *felt* like saying yes. I feared, however, that the dream would crash in record time. I'd be that girl: on a terrace in Tahiti, pale in black lingerie, crying into my coffee and papaya, bawling from one end of the honeymoon to the other. Stranded for life with a man I didn't really know, which turns any Eden into hell.

While I worked the next few days, I thought of all the loves I'd imagined over the years, all the men who didn't exist whom I'd desired. I remembered my Fifth Avenue fantasy, in which we were subversive socialites, like F. Scott and Zelda, swinging from chandeliers and losing our minds. In my Las Vegas dream, we drove our white Ferrari, miniature Doberman in my lap, from pawnshop to casino to presidential suite. I'd bought into the Calvin Klein Eternity fantasy: the handsome family in a landscape of sand and cashmere and snow.

I'd held out for the stockbroker with the heart of gold, the cattle rancher with a taste for Proust. I'd dreamed in abstract: baseball players, surfers, Navy Seals, Japanese gangsters. I'd dreamed in pairs: Butch Cassidy and the Sundance Kid, Luke and

Owen. I'd managed to pine after dead men: Chet Baker, Steve McQueen. For Christ's sake, my whole life I'd had a crush on Huckleberry Finn, who was, first of all, a child and, second of all, a character in a book. I'd imagined that Kai would come back, and everything that was wrong with him, which was everything, would be right. I might have denied it, but I'd even wished Kelly would fall into money, be struck by the lightning of ambition, become someone he never wanted to be.

And then I reviewed my reality.

Besides Kai, I'd dated a bulimic man who, after a big meal, slept with Skoal in his lip to puke effortlessly in the night. Learned it on the college wrestling team.

I'd dated an amphetamine freak. He'd get to the bar before me, order anything I might have wanted, from martini to rum and Coke, and have all six or seven drinks lined up on the table.

A one-night stand who lived in Red Hook and let his pit bull lick cum off his hand.

A painter who dragged me to yoga and made me smoke on his fire escape in the rain.

The married one was the worst, of course. He turned out to be not only married but keeping his other girlfriend in a studio in the building where he lived with his family. And the girlfriend babysat his little boy when he came to me. I discovered this when we walked out of my building one golden afternoon, starved from sex, holding hands, and a white Nissan idled on my curb. A kid sat in the driver's lap and practically crawled out the window when he saw Dave.

"I'm sorry, baby," the woman said around the struggling child. "He was so upset he was hyperventilating."

On my first date with Yves, I was in it for filet mignon and Barolo, and I'd perversely been looking forward to tempting then disappointing him. I'd had some cat-and-mouse game in mind. I expected him to be pompous. Instead he told stories about blind-drunk karaoke in Tokyo, his grief the night his best friend won Yves's date by standing on a chair to shred gladiolas in the ceiling fan. The red petals spiraled into ladies' laps, wine-glasses, the necks of men's shirts. He showed me cufflinks made for him by a Hong Kong hotelier: binoculars, in honor of a night Yves fell down opera-house steps.

Listening to him, I forgot myself. Rapt, I propped my cheek on one hand, watched as he carved a dollhouse that floated above the table; each room was a story. His Adam's apple rattling.

That night he'd ordered me a Town Car outside the restau-rant, overpaid the driver, and didn't even kiss me good night. Instead he hugged me, held on after I'd tried to pull away, until my body relaxed, and his warmth seeped through my clothes. At first I was busy formulating the mocking story I'd tell Belinda, but when his warmth reached me, I was comforted to the bone. It was everything I could do to get the car to drive off before I started crying.

Walking home from work, I passed the hooker whose forehead was marked where the stitches had been removed. She was sit-ting on the hood of a car with another woman. The wind biting. She was nodding in the cold.

Inside that scarred, befouled, gray-skinned shell, her soul could have been seeing paradises that would make us all cry. Trees plump with pomegranates, fields scarlet with poppies, and an aquamarine sky. Everyone we'd ever lost was alive, love was free, strangers kissed, their mouths sweet as candy, arms and legs golden and strong and unmarked. Puppies and kittens chased one another, and a naked man came forward, bearing one white rose whose center was infinite, blooming petal after petal after petal. Under bruised eyelids, the orbs of the girl's eyes chased a butterfly.

That night, instead of dreaming, I lay awake to think long and hard about dreaming.

My mother debilitated rapidly. We didn't speak for two precious weeks after she officially refused the operation. The surgery was more likely to damage than to help, but it had been her only chance. She insisted she didn't want anyone "breaking into her."

"What the fuck do you mean?" I asked, crying hysterically.

She called every day. "Do you still love me?"

"What do you mean?"

"I just want you to say yes, Lee."

"Mom, what are you talking about, for Christ's sake?"

Her fate sealed then, we decided to visit Carmel. An aunt of hers had never stopped talking about her vacations there, and my mother couldn't let it go. When I picked her up in Bridge-hampton, I smoked outside while she packed as carefully as if we were flying to heaven, not California. I stared at a clover bud, its curved ivory spears converging to form a ball: it looked like a plant grown on Saturn.

This sense of being a foreigner to my own planet increased during our walk in the state park on our second day. We were in a bad science-fiction film. A cove of blue Lucite was sheltered by bluffs of eucalyptus, the plants sucking into cliffs' crevices. Octopus arms of weed trailing as water climbed onto white sand and fell back. Sluglike otters we took for dead were suddenly resurrected by cold turquoise waves that lost color as they washed up. A goose waddled with chartreuse goslings, the mother's stare obsidian, aristocratic, ruthless.

Since we'd gotten on the plane, we'd been fighting. *How much do we tip the cabdriver? I don't know, eight dollars. That's too much. Then why did you ask?* I wanted room service; she wanted breakfast downstairs. She wanted to bring umbrellas on our walk; I didn't think it would rain.

We meant something else, of course. *How dare you leave me? Well, how dare you let me go? You seem to want to go so you'll never be disappointed again in this world. How do you know, when you're too afraid to ask me? I think you're rushing to darkness. But will you still love me? What do you mean?*

I was livid, convinced on some level she was relieved to escape the burden of her dreams. And it was true that after I'd left our life together, my mother finished fewer and fewer of the things she'd started. As if without me, the blue jay feathers and snowbells lost purpose. Even her house smelled a bit of compost.

We stood on the cliff, looked over the wild sea. We stood side by side, shielding eyes with hands. We looked at the horizon, and there was nothing there. I'd turn to say something, but when she'd look, I'd turn away. When I looked back, she turned away.

God, this legacy she gave me, this legacy I took from her. Our poor halfway souls. And our sad midway love—her up there, me down here. I wanted to go back to that cliff, more than anything in the world, and take her small shoulders in my hands and turn her to me.

FIVE

◇◇◇◇◇

"*I suppose you think I'm one of those hysterical girls who are always threatening suicide. That only shows you don't know me at all. I've never ever made up my mind to kill myself before; I've scarcely even considered it. Because I think it's a madly tiresome thing to do, and the only possible excuse for making such a nuisance of yourself is to wait until you're quite quite certain you want to. Then you're pretty sure to do it properly. Until yesterday evening, there was always something left to stop me from being certain—some tiny little thing, like feeling curious about a movie we were going to see, or about what I'd eat for dinner, or just what was going to happen next. Well, yesterday I suddenly found I'd come to the end of all that.*"

"*How do you mean?*"

"*I just knew I'd come to the end. It happened in a bar on Sunset Boulevard, way downtown, in the middle of the evening. I caught my own eye in the mirror and I looked at myself—not the way you usually do—really looked. The bar was crowded, but I might just as well have been alone on a desert island; that was how I felt. I knew this must be the end, because I saw that now I'm not good for anything—anything at all.*"

—CHRISTOPHER ISHERWOOD, from *Down There on a Visit*

Yves sat in my orange chair, legs crossed at the ankle, scotch held in the air. I perched on his lap, piling gold lamé on my knees. I looked around the place. I'd accepted Yves's proposal the week before, and tonight I planned on telling everyone. Gray afternoon exploded into purple evening.

"Oh, Yves, this might suck," I whined.

"Have another drink," he said, shifting legs under me in obvious pain. "Only way to kill the jitters, Lee."

We had both decided to forget the only other time he'd come here. I'd made dinner but overcooked the lamb because he was late, driving in circles. He wouldn't say, but I don't think he was lost; he just couldn't believe it was the right neighborhood, with the graffiti, burned cars, live-poultry shops.

We ate by candlelight so he wouldn't see the grimy walls, but darkness, of course, invited roaches. He devoted his body language to seeming relaxed, but I caught him wiping grease from his wineglass, crunching a bug under his shoe, sneaking gristle from his mouth. I got despondent, staring at our flicker ing shadows.

"Hey," he'd said, brushing my cheek with his knuckles. "I've got an idea. Apple crumb at Fanelli's to finish the night off."

So we'd driven into the city, and I was silent until we were seated at the bar. He ate dessert. I drank whiskey. And suddenly my poverty and dependence seemed glamorous again. I was the urchin selling violets in the dusk, skin burning anemic, eyes ablaze. He was the stranger in the bowler hat, strolling in the shadows, pennies jingling in pockets.

∞∞∞∞

Friends transform an apartment; it's not unlike watching a sick person gain back weight. The epicenter was the turntable. Through the smoke, bracelets and lips glittered. Men leaned in thresholds. My friends looked wild, with diamond eyebrow studs and pink hair and tattooed necks and hand-sewn shirts. Why had I forgotten the impression they made? It had been a long time since I'd thrown a party. I kept checking Yves's reaction, but his expression didn't stray from generic benevolence.

A Chihuahua trotted between shoes, hair cut into a full-body mohawk. Giuseppe put a cocktail napkin over its head: "Look! An Amish puppy!"

Audrey sat back in her chair, seltzer clasped in hands, and observed beatifically. At one point, Ozzie pressed his ear to her belly. I overheard him telling her to name the kid Ozzie.

Kelly sat cross-legged on the floor, sifting through album jackets. Cheeks pink, hair damp, blue hooded sweatshirt with the words "South Beach" in white. The tip of a tattoo extended beyond the sleeve.

Jamie bartended, concocting custom cocktails. She tottered over, pressed a sticky glass into my hand.

"This is a little something I call the Bombay Hooker."

"Dare I ask what's in it?"

She looked at me for a moment. "Old family recipe. Kind of sacred," she said, and went back to work.

"You have no idea what you put into it," I accused her.

"That's what I meant," she called from the kitchen.

The Israeli boys sat in the kitchen, pale faces trying for indifference. They watched Vanessa snort a line off a bald stranger's head, then nodded in time as she danced.

Sherry fell asleep on the toilet, red mouth open, lavender panties around ankles, black thigh gleaming. I said her name, and she started, wiped her eyes lazily, cute as a Vargas girl.

The only friend who didn't come was Belinda.

⬦⬦⬦⬦⬦

Yves spent most of the night sitting, tumbler in hand, smiling like a sphinx. He rarely got up, and when he did, it was to peruse books or freshen his drink. Once, he offered a handkerchief to Jamie when Sherry, swing dancing, bumped her drink.

Reflected in the Empire mirrors of his eyes, the clumsy lot of fools: maraschino cherry between teeth, white lines on a mirror, Vanessa's red fishnets, a black hand holding a pimiento olive.

I cleared my throat, the speech ticker-taping through my head. I was poised to clink the martini shaker with silver stirrer. Gazing onto faces, I knew my ears were turning scarlet.

Sweat beaded my upper lip. I was floating, pressed to the ceiling like an astronaut, looking down on my own self. I could actually see the middle part down my red head. The lavender valley between my big white tits. Crimson toenails peeking from under the gold hemline.

"I feel like your chaperone," Yves said, having come up beside me.

"What?" I said. "Oh, please, you can drink these kids under the table."

"Not tonight," he said. "I think I'm still tired. Would you call me a car?"

"No! If you leave, I'm going with you."

"Let me go home gracefully. Let me call it a night."

No one had known that I planned on making an announcement, not even Yves, although he must have suspected that was why I had the party. He did look tired, like someone off a red-eye flight. How like me, to hold a celebration but fail to provide the reason. Suddenly I was nauseated by how many things I'd never completed. I knew I should tell everyone now, but I also knew the words would not come out of my mouth. Instead I apologized to Yves, and he waved me away.

"For what, Lee? Have a good time. Have fun."

Jamie and Vanessa jumped around to Devo, and Martine told an endless story to Tyrone, who was rolling a blunt. The dog licked a piece of cheese on the kitchen floor.

Sherry was lap dancing over Marcus, who was passed out.

The bald stranger sketched Sherry and Marcus on a paper bag.

Candle wax dripped off the table. Records everywhere. Cigar extinguished in coconut drink. Chico cha-cha-chaed up to me, asked what the party had been for, anyway.

"Oh, nothing," I said. "A very merry unbirthday to you."

A crew left for Blondie's. Red wine spilled on shag carpet. Record skipping. I took off my shoes and kissed people good-bye.

The Israeli boys were the only guests left, playing quarters in the kitchen.

Besides Kelly, who sat in the butterfly chair, beer can between thighs. Shoulders broad as eagle's wings. Ringlets fallen from the elastic. Plump lips, like he'd been eating sour candy. He didn't look ready to leave.

I wrapped a ratty turquoise afghan around my shoulders and sat on the floor next to him. The downstairs boys, hands in pockets, filed past us. They morosely thanked me. I asked Kelly if he wanted another beer.

"I haven't finished this one," he said.

"You've had it forever. I'm sure it's warm." I said I'd make a nightcap.

"Are you kicking me out?" he asked.

"Of course not."

I mixed us Kahlúa and milk. He said nothing while I made drinks. My back burned, and I was blushing when I sat down. I spilled a bit of drink, licked it off my hand.

"So, what do you want to know about me?" he asked.

"What?" I scoffed.

"Come on, you ask me one question, I ask you one."

"Why are you here?" I asked.

"In New York or in your apartment?"

"Either one," I said, smoothing the dress over my thighs.

"I'll answer both. I'm here for two reasons. One, because my friend hanged himself in our motel room." He pulled off his sweatshirt, standing hairs on end with static. "And, how should I say, it forced me to look at my life. I decided I had to come here to find someone I know, prove something to her."

"I'm sorry about your friend," I said, looking into my drink.

He sipped. "And I'm here in your apartment because I wanted to talk to you, like this, and you've been avoiding me. My turn."

"Shoot."

"Do you know you're one of the unhappiest girls I've ever known?"

I stood to refill my drink, to hide my face. My hands shook as I poured Kahlúa over ice. My eyes blurry.

His hands on my hips, lips on my neck, one hand pushing away my hair. I stood like a statue, my drink in my hands, eyes wide open, rigid. Hot breath on cool back. I closed my eyes, let my head roll back to lay on his shoulder. I turned my face to his mouth.

I moved to face him. He held handfuls of gold, we stumbled

without going anywhere, the record ended. I clung to his belt loops, then wrapped my hand around the back of his neck, bit his lower lip. We swayed like marathon dancers.

I pulled off his T-shirt. Kissed the meat of his arm. We fell onto the couch, and I was covered, smothered, the world gone dark. His back was wide, unmeasurable by my hands.

My eyes closed, visions flickered: the surf, a scorpion, Kelly's hand around vodka bottle, his eyes the day of the suicide train, a man hanging, a palm leaf.

We revolved, lay side by side, his hand held my breast through the gold, rubbed nipple with thumb. Hardness in his jeans against my belly. He was long enough to show above his waistband, and I swiped the pearl off the tip, licked my finger. His hand climbed my inner thigh, then cupped me.

I gathered my skirt, pulling up gold, pushing down panties, and we looked into each other's eyes. Our eyes were close in the shadows, wet, dilated. The crackle of condom wrapper. I waited, watched.

He rolled on top, put just the head in, and paused. I could feel his heartbeat down there. That alone was almost too much. Suddenly he was in to the hilt. He barely had to move. Closer to the end, I wanted more. Imagined him with the power to be where he was and in my mouth at the same time, like a unicorn.

Later, in my bed, I took the head in my mouth and held the rest with my hand, blood thumping under my thumb. I was on my knees at a right angle to his body, his hand between my legs. His hand kept trying, but lapsing, forgetting. His breath hard, bottom lip pushed out.

The halter of my dress pulled down to waist, the skirt of it pulled up, to make a big gold belt.

A crescendo of bad words and a throat full of buttermilk.

We lay there, flung like the dead onto the bed. The room was dark, but he was darker. Inside his silhouette, fireflies bumped and glowed.

I slipped out of his stout arms the next morning. Wrapped fur coat around dress, pulled on cowboy boots. At the bodega, I bought eggs, bacon, bread, coffee, cream.

In the apartment, Kelly was stretching his arms above his head, his face marked by sheets. Semihard in blue jeans. He pulled on his sweatshirt and swaggered over, took my face in his hands and kissed me hard.

"I got breakfast," I said, looking down, blushing.

"I'm going for a quick jog."

"In what? Jeans and work boots?"

He smacked his hands together and grinned like a lunatic. "You better believe it. Wake this body up."

I watched him out my window. He jogged in place waiting for the Driggs traffic to clear, then took off in the pink morning light. I yelled not to get lost, and he waved, put his hood up like a boxer. I laughed, shook my head.

I fried the bacon, planning to cook eggs in its fat. I whisked cream into the eggs. Lay bread under the broiler but waited to turn it on. I set out plates, sang along with Francoise Hardy.

He was glistening and beaming when he stomped in, and he inhaled deeply. Said it was the most beautiful perfume in the world. I smiled as he kissed my neck.

"Breakfast in an evening gown," he said, breaking bacon from under the paper towel. "That's why I like you, Lee."

I wanted to say: "That's a good enough reason, I guess," but my mouth was dry.

I pushed eggs onto plates with a spatula, pulled out toast, divided bacon. He was sitting at the table, napkin tucked into his shirt, pouring sugar into his coffee.

"Hey," he said after a few minutes, words muffled by a bite of toast. "Can I ask you a personal question?"

I licked strawberry jam off the knife, laughed. "That's funny."

"What?" His eyes widened.

"Well, I think I can handle a question considering I had your—"

He held up a finger. "I see where you're going. Point taken," he said. "Do you and Yves, I mean, you two don't seem to have that much in common."

I looked at him. "That's not a question."

"How serious are you guys?"

"Oh, come on," I said, getting up for coffee. "That's a boring conversation."

"Really. I want to know."

"I mean, I'm going to marry the guy." I held the pot over his cup. "Do you want more?"

The longer he looked at me, the pinker his cheeks turned. I poured him coffee even though he hadn't answered. I didn't want to be looked at anymore. He wasn't exactly single: if anything, this woman sounded more precious to him than Yves would ever be to me. And yet here I was, feeling like the sinner.

"I have to clean," I said, slumping in a chair.

"Lee," he said in a new voice. "I didn't mean—"

I shook my head.

"Can I help you—"

"No. I want to do it alone."

He put on his jacket slowly, came and kissed me where I sat. I let him but didn't get up.

◇◇◇◇◇

After I vacuumed up ash and cherry stems and peanuts, I poured a scotch and ran a bath. I was sore, and lowered myself into the hot water carefully. My dress lay on the kitchen floor. A puddle of gold.

They forgot to teach us in school that the responsible thing, eventually, was to let go of dreams. They let us believe it was noble to pursue the impossible. They left us to discover compromise on our own. Compromise was the golden password, I was learning, to adulthood.

Yves was compromising. No way I satisfied all his requirements. But he was getting older and finally knew in his heart that he was mortal, and I was exciting to keep around. I once waited uptown for a taxi, smoking a cigarette. The orange-and-white-haired doorman, in red uniform, told me a secret after we watched a woman exit a limousine with a cat's crate: he lived in Bay Ridge and had owned an ocelot for seven years.

"It's illegal, you know," he'd said, and I'd never forgotten the pride in his tone.

And it would be a luxurious arrangement for me. Already, a loft was forming in my mind: an aquarium of piranhas, a mink quilt, a Philips flat-screen TV. I could get that powder-blue daybed I'd always bragged about, recline all day, eating bonbons and watching soap operas. When Yves came home from work, I'd give him a blowjob before he could put his briefcase down.

I wasn't entirely sure how we'd entertain ourselves until we died. Maybe he could start being strict with money, and I would be forced to become duplicitous. I could become a textbook alcoholic and do things like stash whiskey in the laundry hamper. I could cheat extravagantly and charge rooms at the St. Regis to his card. I could show up at his friend's office in a lace teddy under a raincoat. We could become swingers. We could become obsessed with Tibet. I could get plastic surgery to look like a panther.

I drew the line at parenting and fund-raising.

On my days off, I paged through bridal magazines. All the girls looked like cheap princesses. What I really wanted, I told Yves, while I reclined on the couch sipping wine one night, was an elegant rave. He laughed, half listening, half watching CNN.

"No, really," I said. "Some warehouse we can trash, good drugs, an insane DJ, roses and gardenias scattered all over the cement floor."

"My dear, you can have whatever you want."

"And I want to invite as many people as possible, to get as many gifts as I can."

I decided to register at Neiman Marcus so I could eventually exchange china and silver for clothes and shoes.

"And our honeymoon?" Yves asked.

"A suite at the Carlyle here in the city. For a week. Room-service cheeseburgers, cartoons, martinis. And dirty sex in a gold-framed mirror."

On the day I'd planned on accepting Yves's proposal, I asked him to take me for a walk in Central Park under a chilly pink sun. But I couldn't get my courage together until we had walked all the way down to the seaport. I chattered, holding his hand then taking mine away, then grabbing his again. Finally, I stopped under a wooden mermaid. The sidewalk iridescent with scales, and stinking. Stuck my gum under a public phone. Breathed deeply, then spoke.

We'd then spent that afternoon at a seaport pub, showing my ring, which Yves had been keeping in his eyeglass case, to barflies. The windows, tall as doors, were open to the cold sun. The wooden bar gleamed from years of oily palms. Yves didn't say "This is the beginning, love," or "It will be good, you'll see," and I silently thanked him. We sat on stools, under ceiling fans, and bantered with the bartender. After a couple beers, a bottle of Freixenet was plunked down. The bartender indicated three men on the other side of the bar as he unwrapped foil. It was a sweet thing to be toasted by strangers, even with bad champagne.

Yves said we had to clean up my finances since being married would legally join mine with his, and he couldn't risk being audited. When his accountant, out of alarm, I think, faxed my credit report, Yves poured a straight scotch and unbuttoned his shirt. He put on bifocals and sat at the kitchen table for a while before speaking. I flitted about in the background, waiting to be addressed.

Finally he cleared his throat, took off his glasses. "Come on in and have a seat, Lee," he said, patting the chair next to him.

"What's up?" I said cheerfully.

"More than anything else, I'm just interested, not upset, just interested in how you racked up these numbers."

"Well, let's see," I said in my most casual, professional voice, pulling the pages to me. "Uh, that Discover card, that whole balance, was a trip to St. Barth's, from a while ago. I got the card because I didn't have any money. And I never paid it off, so I guess it's been earning, uh, interest ever since."

"And overlimit fees, late fees, and finance charges."

"Right," I said slowly. "All of that. But it was an awesome trip. And I really needed to get away."

He smiled tightly at me.

"Uh, that there was totally not my fault. I had a motorcycle accident in Massachusetts, and I didn't have any health insurance, so . . . whatever. They charged me for everything. The ambulance, the doctor, all that stuff they're not supposed to charge you for."

Abruptly, he took the document back. "I think it's better,

maybe, if I just take care of this. I think it's better if we don't go through all seven pages of vacations and accidents."

"It's up to you, babe. I can explain everything."

"That's what I'm afraid of, to be honest."

We walked through SoHo differently, as if we belonged to each other. We went to Raoul's, and I watched him watch me across the bar. I winked and blew a kiss. Even lying in bed, reading, a parasol of intimacy opened. We were varnished with promises like a sugar-glazed cake. These new circumstances felt tenuous, but perhaps real life was tenuous and I was just learning that I had to learn to be comfortable. All the unlikely dreams had been released, like a cage of doves.

But when I didn't meditate hard enough, Kelly showed up in my mind and burst like a cowboy through saloon doors, his silhouette looming. The setting sun broke around his huge arms and between his legs, beams shooting from the edges of his torso. With one hand he spun his gun, broke a bottle with the other.

Then, one dark, cold morning, Yves and I had a mishap. I sat on the edge of the bed, glared at periwinkle and black clouds. Determined to be adult, I tried to make light of it instead of punishing him with silence. I might have said something like: "Maybe you better look into Viagra or something, honey, because we have a lot of mornings in our future." And I might have pinched his cheek.

Later, he was straightening his cuffs as I zippered teal kitten-heeled boots up my legs, and I reminded him to give me money before he left for the day. As the cash changed hands, he smiled, kissed my cheek, and asked if I wouldn't mind collecting my receipts from now on.

"The accountant," Yves explained, rubbing a lint brush on his slacks. "He's compulsive, Lee."

That day, I lit a smoke at the bar as the lunch crowd thinned, nodded as people put on coats and picked teeth and left. My mouth wouldn't smile. In the ladies' room, I pawed though the empty gram bags in my purse until I found a plump one. Josh uncorked bottles and thrust them into ice. The street turned blue and the restaurant gold.

When Kelly appeared through the glass door, I straightened up, slipped my ring into my pocket. He wore a black ski jacket with blond fur-lined hood. I'd arranged both of our shifts so we hadn't seen each other since he'd left my apartment, and although he'd called my phone, I never picked up.

He approached warily, hands in pockets. "What's up, Lee."

"Do you want to go on a field trip?"

At first he declined. But a look must have passed over my face, sad or desperate or both, because he suddenly agreed to meet the next morning.

Pearly sun and cold air passed through the glass of the train's window. I looked at Kelly, body barely jiggling, head tipped against seat, crow's-feet carved even in sleep. His mouth closed, hands laced in lap.

The train was almost empty. Backyards blurred through trees. Above-ground pools, tarps sagging with rainwater and orange leaves. Dogs asleep in yellow grass. A flagstone porch crowded with paper bags of bottles and cans. In strip malls, people loaded cars in slow motion; the train moved fast enough to slow down the world. Here and there, a junkyard. A big lot crammed with school buses. Cars in line waiting for us to pass, waiting for the red-and-white-striped gates to spring up. They were waiting to get on with their lives. But of course, here in suburbia, I had that old suspicion no one was doing anything important. They might as well move slowly and wait in lines because their endeavors were cheap, provincial, scattered.

"It's my mother's birthday," I said when he woke up.

"How old is she?" he asked blearily.

"She's dead," I said, pawing through my bag for lipstick.

In the cab, passing horses in fields, cornflowers, Kelly patted me clumsily. His hand dwarfed my knee. He said we should stay in separate rooms.

"What?" I said, confused.

"I just think it's a good idea."

He put his hair in a ponytail as I watched him, and he made a show of craning to look at the landscape.

"Beautiful out here," he said.

The house's whitewashed brick glowed in the dark afternoon. The rosiness showed through the paint as if the house were blushing. The yard was clotted with leaves, and the air smelled of decay and sky and burning wood. We'd come from a place with only industrial smells to one so heavy with fragrance: the world here took on meaning by virtue of the air's weight.

By the door, the bush had pushed out one late rose. Kelly seemed both pleased and shy to have arrived. (Modesty had been a theme at Penn Station; I awkwardly bought his train ticket, he fetched me coffee.) Walking up the path, Kelly carried both bags, leaves crackling underfoot. We were like old-fashioned newlyweds. The way he gestured for me to enter first was tender and quiet.

I didn't want to invade the house too quickly, so I resisted turning on lights. It was urgent we move slowly and carefully, as though someone were sleeping in the bedroom.

The house was shadowy, the air dense with days elapsed. Dead bees on windowsills. I opened windows, and shadows seemed to stir as air moved through the rooms now.

The mantelpiece was white. Above it hung an oval mirror splotched with what looked like black frost. The hollow of the hearth pungent with ash.

Propped on the mantel, leaning against the wall, was a painting I'd done when I was little. The dancer wore a tutu, a tiara that looked like cupcake icing instead of diamonds, red corsages at breast and wrist. White arms reaching to the sky. Crimson smudge of mouth.

My mom used to look at it all the time, scanning the ballerina's face, her tutu, the electric-blue folds of stage curtain.

"I just love it," she'd say. "I don't know why, but I do. I just love it."

And here was Kelly, looking at it as if he might know the ballerina from somewhere and was trying to recall her name.

I was sitting in an armchair, looking at the floor, when Kelly asked which room he should take. I showed him to what had been my room. The rough-hewn bed was painted yellow. A bedside bureau crudely painted white. I turned on the blue milk-glass lamp, spotlighting a dish that held an earring back, a safety pin, a cherry pit. The bed was naked.

"We have to kind of forage for sheets and stuff. I don't really know what's where, actually," I said with some anxiety.

"Don't worry, we'll find something," he said in a very calm voice. "Let's eat first."

"I don't know what we're going to eat."

"Can we walk anywhere from here?"

I shook my head. We could call a cab. I hadn't really thought about any of this. I was staring forlornly out the window when he asked if I had a bicycle.

"In the shed. But it will take you forever to get to the grocery store."

"That sounds like a challenge," he said.

It didn't take forever, but it took a long time. I was smoking in the kitchen when I heard bicycle wheels crunch gravel. The squeak of a kickstand. The crumple of grocery bags lifted from the basket. His cheeks were bright, like apples, and his hair wild.

The only bottle I hauled from the bag was sparkling cider. I held it up, squinting from the smoke of the cigarette clenched between my teeth.

"This the best you could do?" I asked, half joking.

He broiled steaks while I looked for liquor in the basement. Found a dusty-shouldered handle of Canadian Club next to the lawn mower. The kitchen smelled good when I came upstairs. A salad of tomato and purple onion sat on the table, next to a round of sourdough bread on a cutting board.

After dinner, we sat at the table, me leaning forward once in a while to ash. A moth bumped itself into the bulb of the table lamp. The lamp's red base cast a pinkness on our faces. There had been no plan when I'd decided to come out here. I was waiting for something to happen.

I sipped my neat whiskey, tapped my cigarette, looked from

the moth to Kelly, and back again. His face was placid, the wide planes smooth and shining. He stared at the light, arms crossed. Cicadas outside became louder and louder, the silence inside deeper and deeper.

He finished his cider. "I'm beat," he announced, and collected the plates. When he started rinsing things, I said I'd do that, he'd done enough.

He smiled over his shoulder: "I got it covered."

I lit a new cigarette, listened to him quietly rummage in hall closets. Through the turquoise scrim of the screen door, a beetle showed his glossy underside to me, his barbed components working together as he climbed from left to right.

I was bewitched by my own solitude, and sat for an hour. Felt the cocaine and whiskey hushing down. I can't say I had any thoughts. I don't think I felt many feelings. The kitchen was suspended in the night, a room with a red lamp, an ashtray full of crushed butts, a garbage can with a rind of bread and two T-bones.

When I went up to my mother's room, I saw that Kelly had found sheets and a tartan blanket, and had made her bed for me. His door was closed.

I woke to light coming through bamboo blinds in razor strips. My breath made steam. I didn't want to get out of bed. Ever.

Kelly opened my door after softly rapping a few times. He held a spatula, greasy with egg bits. Sat on the edge of the bed.

"Morning," he said, and he sounded like a farmer.

The blanket was pulled to just under my eyes, and I stared at him.

"All you have to do," he said benignly, "is crawl into the kitchen. Eggs, cold steak, hot coffee. All you have to do, Lee, is get up, and I'll do the rest."

I kept staring. Finally he peeled the blanket from my face, pried it from my hands. I'd slept in yesterday's clothes.

"You don't even have to get dressed, girl. You have no excuse."

I couldn't smile, but I did pull myself to a sitting position and then put one foot and the other on the floor. Combed my crazy hair with my fingers, looked at him as if to ask if I was acceptable. He licked his palm, pressed down what must have been a few errant strands.

"I need a cigarette," I croaked.

Light rippled in the cold kitchen. I gobbled eggs with a burning cigarette in the other hand. Holly leaves tapped against the window in the wind, and sounded like fingernails. I kept looking to see who was there.

Kelly's hair was wet, raked into a neat braid. Shetland sweater, blue jeans. With his back to me, he started another pot of coffee.

"I woke up one morning," I told him, and he turned around, "a few months ago. I'd been at Black Betty the night before, this bar in Brooklyn. Anyway. It was Brazilian night, and I did a bunch of coke with this kid, but whatever. That's actually not the point."

I took a long drag. Kelly stood, back against sink, big hands loosely gripping counter's edge, waiting.

"I woke up," I resumed, "and it's not that I wanted to die. It's that I knew for a fact that I *was* dying. Up until that morning, I'd been living. Maybe not a wholesome and productive life"—quick drag—"but living. Now that I'm dying, I almost want to speed up the process. I sure as hell don't know how to slow it down, and I'm pretty sure there's no way to get back to where I was before."

Slowly he dried his hands on a dishrag. I smoked and watched him. He picked up our mugs and refilled them with steaming coffee. Set them down at the table, then sat across from me. Squinted at the ceiling for a moment, arms crossed. Then he looked at me.

"Okay," he said. "First of all, I have to say this—I think you're melodramatic."

I made some noise of protest, or shock. He just shrugged.

"You are," he insisted calmly. "Which is a symptom of imagination, and thus a good thing. You're also totally self-involved."

I just stared with mouth open, cigarette burning between fingers.

"Again," he said, "the sign of someone who can create a world, who can mythologize everything."

Then he reached across the table and folded one of my hands in both of his. "That said, I do believe you're dying, and I know all about that; I know it inside and out. I can tell you everything you never wanted to know."

I tore my hand from his, gaped at him with horror. I couldn't believe how open I'd made myself. He seemed slightly amused, only fueling my indignation.

"You stupid fuck," I said, standing up.

"Come on now," he said, straightening his face.

"You tricked me." I ran into my mother's room and slammed the door.

I put up a decent fight. Even moved the bureau in front of the lockless door. Scowled at everything he said, my arms crossed and shoulders raised to earlobes, like an angry brat. The morning sun had been snuffed by clouds. I paced around the dark room. Thought of dropping out the window into the bleached hydrangea, but then what? My wallet was in the kitchen.

When I finally emerged, he was in the kitchen, tying a bundled quilt onto his back.

"You ready?" he asked.

"For what?" I scoffed.

"A nice long hike."

"Hell no." I grabbed a chair and sat down heavily.

"So you're just going to hang out here with no food or cigarettes?"

"I have cigarettes."

"No," he said, tapping his homemade backpack, "I do."

A surreal landscape of sloping farm squares adjacent to the sodded lawns of summer mansions. Traffic was sparse; a Lamborghini roared around a tractor.

Pewter clouds hung low. The darkness was thrilling, but I didn't want to give in. Without being wet, houses and rhododendrons and cornfields were endowed with the lushness of bad weather. A hardy cosmos leaned from a tuft of straw. I walked behind him, throwing rocks and sticks into the hedges, and sometimes missing him by an inch. Kelly walked like a man on an unhurried pilgrimage.

"It's going to rain, asshole," I said.

"Good," he said without turning around.

Wide space narrowed to an intimate neighborhood with green-shuttered white houses close to the road, privet trimmed tight, a lighted window. In one yard, a white-bearded Labrador staggered arthritically toward us, his deep and throaty warning almost inaudible.

"It's okay, old boy," Kelly said. "We won't bother you."

The geography flattened, turned briny and grew reeds. We walked past the closed ticket booth, through the deserted parking lot, and climbed the boardwalk stairs. The wind tossed our hair, and I was startled by the sudden hiss of waves, of dune grass. I'd forgotten how sweet the salt smells. At the top of the stairs, we looked at the gray water, the sky, a dark sand stripe that zigzagged parallel to the surf line. A dead tree had washed onto shore, branches like an empty grape cluster. A tire. A yellow gasoline can.

Kelly used our boots to weight the quilt's corners. I was starving, thirsty. We ate hard-boiled eggs, olives, bread, and a chunk of smoked ham we pulled apart with our hands. We passed cider back and forth. I smoked a cigarette while Kelly unwrapped a bar of chocolate. Ash flew in the wind. Hair caught in my mouth.

"When'd you boil eggs, mister Outward Bound?" I asked.

"When you were in your room freaking out."

I laughed. "I'm not angry anymore."

He winked, chewing chocolate.

While he pissed down the beach on wood slats stuck in dune, I lay half on quilt, half in sand. I could feel sand blown into the cuffs of my violet coat, and sifting into my hair. I looked straight into the sky.

"What are you going to do to me?" I asked Kelly when he sank to his knees.

"Nothing. I'll do things *with* you. For you."

"Are you making self-righteous distinctions?"

"Yeah. I guess so."

"But we both belong to other people," I said. I was giddy.

"I don't. Maybe you do. That's your problem."

"You do, too," I protested, sitting up, smacking sand from my hands. "The girl. The girl you came to find."

"Actually, that's not what you think. I should have made that clear from the beginning. I didn't realize how it came across."

I kneeled, dropped a hand on his shoulder. "Just what am I supposed to think?"

"I know, I know," he said.

His face fell, daunted. Wet brown eyes stared at eggshells and olive pits in the sand. I asked him to just tell me.

"I'm going to do better than an explanation," he said.

"What do you mean?"

"Save next Thursday."

"Okay."

He stared at me, as if trying to communicate without words. So I punched him in the shoulder.

"Stop being glum," I said. "You know, *you're* the freak. Not me. You are."

He chased me to the water. Then we followed the surf in and back, getting our feet wet. We combed the beach, throwing skate pods that were shiny like leather coin purses. I worked the tangerine hinge of a crab claw. It was a sweet home video, until rain fell.

Walking down dark, cold, hushed lanes. The rain never picked up. Huge, intermittent drops that splashed when they hit the road. As we passed through the populated stretch, Kelly stopped to read a cardboard sign stapled to a telephone pole.

"Check this out," he said.

I read the sign. "I dare you to go in."

He looked at me. "It's too late. It's dinnertime."

I snorted. "Whatever."

"Fine. I'll go, but you're coming with me."

"Deal. I love strangers' houses."

A cone of light shone on the porch, deifying winged insects. A woman with butter-yellow hair down to her shoulders answered the door. Black turtleneck, black jeans, red lipstick and toenails. White wine. Probably forty, she smiled like a twenty-year-old— quickly, warmly, contagiously.

"I hope we're not interrupting dinner," Kelly said.

"We saw the sign about free kittens," I said.

"Did you?" she asked enthusiastically. "Come right in. Of course you're not interrupting."

We drank wine with Christine on her screened porch. The floor was Astroturfed. The house smelled like hamburger, and bleached prints from museums hung in cheap brass frames. At the far end of the porch, fabric dangled from a sewing machine. A stringy-haired blond kid, whose gender I couldn't determine, Rollerbladed with a Pop-Tart. Children sauntered around in pajamas, dripped off furniture, made vague complaints but didn't pursue them. Through this, Christine sat sideways on her glider, feet up on the arm, unperturbed.

We told her about our beach picnic. She pointed out a gazebo her husband, Jason, was building for her in the backyard. Its skeleton loomed useless and ghostly in the dark. But I had a feeling Jason loved her, and I realized I liked Christine.

"This is my favorite little girl," she said, knees cracking as she squatted to the box of newspaper shreds. She'd decided it was time for me to hold a white kitten with blue eyes. "All the others just run around, careening and wrestling, tussling, and this princess sits tight. She just likes to be held."

As we walked home, Kelly kept looking at the sky, almost stumbling, his head tipped so far back.

"My God, you can see all the stars out here," he said.

"People always say that when they haven't been out of the city in a while," I said, but kindly.

A warm thing cowered in my coat.

At home, Kelly plugged a transistor radio into the outlet above the stove. We sat on the linoleum floor, me in a black slip and Kelly's sweater, him in jeans and long-john shirt. Listened to country music, laughed as the kitten chased a tinfoil ball that we batted back and forth. Laughed till we almost cried. I don't even know why, but it had something to do with the drunken way she ran, weaving, tripping on her own feet, swaying and staring with confusion when she stopped.

"Did you know you were going to take one home when you went in there?" he asked.

"Fuck no." I sighed, pulling hair from my hot face. "This is an accidental kitten."

I knocked the ball under the table, and she pawed it back out.

"Oh, she's tired," he said as she staggered and collapsed against my black silk thigh.

Kelly tucked us into bed, putting water and food on the floor. I asked what would happen if I rolled over in my sleep. I was afraid of killing her.

"It's not going to happen, trust me."

She slept on the pillow, curled into my neck's hollow. I was exhausted, the soles of my feet black from the dirty floors, my hair full of sand, my cheeks windburned. But I had trouble sleeping, electrified by her plush white fur next to my jaw. Her body rattled with dreamy breaths, contented. She already believed I was her mother.

SIX

◇◇◇◇◇

The bee emerging
from deep within the peony
departs reluctantly

—Matsuo Bashō

made Yves leave a meeting at the Mercer Kitchen to meet me at his place because Kelly had to work lunch, and separating had triggered a disappointment that made me feel sick. I was panicky. I actually had expected to introduce Kelly to my mother. Did I think she was on a trip? That she would return one day with souvenirs? Hand me hotel stationery, or a duty-free perfume set, or a conch shell, so waxy and perfect it seemed machine-made?

She would have loved to hear about our picnic in bad weather. She would have liked to eat ham with her hands like we'd done. She would have nodded knowingly when I told her how I lay on the beach, letting sand fill the billows of my clothes, and how I could have let the wind bury me with sand. Part of me had expected to tell her these stories. Waiting for Yves in his loft I'd shuddered, hating, as always, to think of her at all. Even the briefest vision, too small to constitute a thought, sent me to a bad place.

Now we watched Angel take in Yves's loft. She blinked blue eyes like a dumb blonde. Then zigzagged across the Persian rug with that drunken, artless swagger. Yves's arms crossed. Face blank.

"Isn't she sweet?" I said. "I mean, seriously. Don't you love her?"

The kitty jumped onto the white Mies Van der Rohe chair. She sniffed the seams.

"Maybe she shouldn't be up there," Yves said.

"She's fine. They can fall ten stories without getting hurt."

"No, I mean"—he gestured—"the chair."

His phone rang; he plugged in his headset and turned away. He stood at the window, tossing a paperweight between hands. Eyes darting back and forth, looking at nothing.

Talking business, he tried to leave the room, but I caught his waist, turned him to look at her. I beamed at him, squeezed. She batted the hanging corner of a throw. Then she sat down, dragged her bum on the wood floor, staring piteously at me.

"Let me call you back," Yves said.

In his car, I played with the stereo. He told me to leave it on classical. I propped a shoe on the tortoiseshell dashboard, and he gestured it down. So I knocked my head against the white leather headrest.

"I'm just saying you should have asked her," Yves said.

"Well she was so *nice*, Yves. I just assumed."

He smiled thinly. "It's not about nice," he said. "I'm sure she was nice. That doesn't mean she gave the cats shots."

"Well, what do you care, anyway? You don't care if she's sick."

"I care," he said, "because I'm going to be late now."

"No one asked you to drive me."

We waited at a stoplight. I watched his eyes search for something that didn't exist in the city: a horizon. Two white girls in jeans and Prada coats walked through red leaves.

"I'm sorry," I said, apologizing for something I hadn't even done yet.

Got off the subway later that afternoon. Black clouds veined the gold sky, like marble. A threat glowed, one that was not as immediate as a storm warning, but rather a vague promise of hardship. The premonition of New York winter.

Litter in the gutter of North Seventh Street. An elderly Italian man loitered on the corner, radio to ear, square black shades obscuring three quarters of his face, wisps of white hair blown straight up by wind. It was too cold to stand outside: he was pretending to enjoy a summer day. I moved through the peach air as if it were the breath of roses. A dramatic silence in Brooklyn.

At work that night, I picked petals from the crease of the reservation book. Angel paced in my imagination, savage and divine as a snow leopard. I bragged about her until Chico made fun of me.

"You're going to start lactating, Lee."

"Who are you? You're about to be a dad!" I protested.

Shannon smirked behind the bar, wiping hands on rag tucked into waist. "Don't become one of those New York women, Lee. Don't get all book club and Pilates and soy milk. You're my favorite fucked-up party girl."

"Gee, thanks."

During the next few hours, in the anxiety of sweet-potato soufflés, on the trays of Cosmopolitans, among the hands and faces of strangers, Angel's image became less distinct.

I got off the subway a bit after 2:00 AM. Ambled down my blue street, mumbling under my breath, still high on work. Opened my door with a hopeful smile.

"I'm home, sugar," I said. "Angel. I'm home."

Left bag and keys on floor, and walked from room to room. When I didn't see her anywhere, I pulled down the comforter, turned over piles of clothes, lifted towels from floor. *Don't panic*, I told myself. I looked in the toilet. I looked in the refrigerator. I checked the hollows of shoes and boots.

"Fuck!" I said, wringing hands. "I knew it."

I was checking cabinets when I noticed. I'd opened the window to dump an ashtray onto the street and hadn't closed it. The gap was four inches. I put my hand over my mouth.

◇◇◇◇◇

Outside, I hunted through shadows. Moved blue recycling bags on the curb. Oh my God, I saw her.

Rushed to the other side of the street. But it was a white napkin caught in wild grass.

Two guys rolled down the sidewalk in Adidas sneakers and hooded sweatshirts. I asked if they'd seen a kitten, held my hands apart to demonstrate size.

"We don't live here," one said.

"Just passing through," said the other. "Sorry."

After circling the block, and the surrounding blocks, I stood in the moonlight and tried to gather my thoughts. *I need to make a sign*, I decided.

Upstairs in my kitchen, I sat at the table with paper and a marker. I couldn't write, though; my fingers were shaking.

Then I heard a scuffle.

Found her behind the stove, caught between pipes.

"Oh my little biscuit," I said, squatting. "My sugarplum, my babycakes."

What is this saccharine nonsense coming out of my mouth?

Stayed up for a while. Angel was like a baby, sleepy in my arms one minute, eyes literally closing as she tried to keep them open, then jumping down and running wild. At one point, she sat in the dark, staring up into the garment rack. Every other minute, she'd rear up and swat at white sequins, miss, wobble, and sit again.

Outside my window, truckers trucked, hookers fucked, cops cruised, kids smoked, elders yelled, invalids slept, spouses fought, lovers kissed, while I watched a pussycat playing with stars in a black room.

⟡⟡⟡⟡⟡

Kelly knocked on my door Thursday, hands stuffed in pockets. Beige vest over white hooded sweatshirt. Wet hair combed down but tucked behind ears. We both had the day off. I told him I felt as if we were going on an undercover assignment, and he laughed. He drove us to Queens in Guy's truck, stealing looks at me as often as he could take his eyes from the road. Angel slept, tucked into my coat.

Outside, the cold, sunny street glittered with cars and strollers and bikes. We stopped at a grocer and bought a baguette, pasta, sauce. Inside the store, an elderly man with a black eye patch leaned on his cane, a *Daily Racing Form* in his hand, talking odds to no one in particular. The guy behind the register apparently recognized Kelly.

"That girl, she eats only spaghetti," he said in a thick Greek accent, relishing the absurdity.

Kelly nodded. "She does; it's crazy."

The guy put an apple into the bag as an afterthought. "Tell her she better take vitamins or something."

The basement apartment was carpeted in white. Single bed, neatly made with a white afghan pulled up to one white pillow. A cheap brass chandelier, the fourth flame-shaped bulb dark. A hot plate, a yellow sponge. Pressed-wood cabinets with white knobs.

We sat on a white pleather couch, facing a window of dead leaves. The only valuable item was the stereo system: Bang & Olufsen speakers, a turntable, big leather earphones on the carpet. Milk crates of records.

Nick's elegant cheekbones were chipped like aged stone. Brown hair parted to the side, with a nimbus of split ends.

She wore a black Fugazi T-shirt and black jeans. Bare feet. No makeup. A white strip of leather tied in a knot around her wrist.

Kelly pointed to the bag beside him on the couch. "You want me to cook for you, Nick?"

"What do you mean," she said. "You think I forgot how to cook or something."

"No, I didn't," Kelly said earnestly. "I like cooking for you."

"One day I'll call you and say, 'Get your ass over here and cook me some spaghetti, Kelly Bradley.' "

"All right." He shrugged. "Deal."

It took her one second too long to process anything, and I had a hard time talking because of the false importance her hesitations gave to everything. It always seemed she was giving my words too much consideration, when actually she was giving them none. I told her how I got the kitten, and she beamed, but when I got to the part about losing her in the apartment, she forgot to stop smiling. Then, when she remembered, her frown was exaggerated.

She was tall and held herself like a retired dancer. If she couldn't finish a sentence, she'd stare at the ceiling, then laugh.

"Oh, shit," she said, looking at me steadily. "Forget it."

For a while, Nick dragged a sock around the carpet for Angel.

"C'mon," she said. "C'mon, little girl."

The kitten would pounce, and Nick would pull the sock farther, taunting. A name was tattooed in turquoise script on the sole of her foot. I was going to ask, but when I opened my mouth, Kelly shook his head.

Chinatown's storefronts bloomed with topaz ducks and were crowned with red neon characters. An unlikely address, but the loft had been available and cheap fifteen years ago when

Guy renovated it. Kelly unlocked a sparse lobby, led us up two flights.

We stood in a studio that was not uncluttered but still clean as a military station. Black material hanging from industrial clippers pooled like lava on the floor. A black toy pistol positioned on a light box. "Ain't Skeered" bumper sticker peeling off filing cabinet. Utility kitchen along one wall.

Prints and contact sheets tacked along the walls. Transformations were conducted here. On a few occasions before tonight, I myself had passed under this window and seen lightning flash through black curtains.

Guy emerged, shirtless, from the bathroom with a newspaper. His white arms so sinewy and muscular, they were grotesque. Shiny black hair to jaw. Jagged brows, and lips like an Italian movie star.

"How's it hanging, Kelly," he said.

Scraggly black hairs between nipples. Black slacks and bare feet. No jewels, no tattoos. But his body was so volatile; his hand reaching out to shake mine was frightening.

I winced like a working-class girl introduced to upper-class parents. After meeting Nick earlier that day, I'd asked to see where Kelly stayed. I knew he lived in Guy's studio, but I'd hoped Guy would have left work and gone back to his own home. He didn't look like the photographs in magazines. He was much uglier or more beautiful, I couldn't decide.

Kelly slept on a single mattress covered with a Mexican blanket in what used to be a supply room. The illicit pleasure I remembered from boarding school of being in a boy's room washed through me for the first time in years. A surfboard leaned in the corner. Blue jeans, a parka with fur hood, and Hawaiian shirts on hangers swayed from white pipe. A copper saucer of patchouli dust on the floor, sticks charred and crossed, next to a cardboard box of clothes.

"She tattooed the name of the guy who did it on the bottom of her foot," he said, lying on his bed, arms crossed behind his head as a pillow.

"If she knew who did it, why didn't she get him arrested?"

"Doesn't work like that there. Not for my crew, at least. We were such assholes, and the Jamaicans hated us."

"Nick was an asshole?"

"No, but she was connected to us, poor thing."

Kelly's vest zipper riding his chin. Tiny dots where mustache and beard would have grown in. That dazed look boys get when they're reclining.

"When my buddy died, you know, in the motel room, I just decided I had to find her. Someone heard she was in New York."

"What did you plan on doing once you found her?" I asked, with a degree of disbelief.

He shrugged, nylon zithered against stubble. "Nothing. I just wanted her to see I hadn't forgotten her. To know that she was important enough to be followed, checked on, consoled. I mean, I'm sure part of my motivation was just guilt. We shouldn't have let her go alone. You know?"

"But you weren't responsible for what happened."

He looked at me quickly. "Not directly. But any one of us could have walked her back that night. And we knew that we should because we were in a weird part of town. But we were stoned and lazy, and she was a tough girl. She took care of herself."

"She was tough?"

"Super tough. She was with this guy Jack for as long as anyone could remember. They were the king and queen. They were so strong. He let her down the worst. He was scared of what had been done, of what he hadn't done, and all that. Basically he didn't understand, and he didn't try. He became a cliché, chasing storms and surfing hurricanes."

I shook my head. "Why couldn't you tell me before?"

"Because it's a private story, Lee. And because it's shameful. To me."

"And it's the most fucking depressing story I ever heard in my life," I said. "No offense."

He smiled. "No offense taken. It is depressing."

"So she just totally lost her shit after," I prodded.

"Well, she'd been depressed, I guess, her whole life. The surfing and hiking and all that were her way of medicating. With endorphins and whatever. Then the incident and the hospital interrupted all that, and, yeah. She lost her shit."

"Same deal with your friend in the motel?"

"Similar. But he'd been on regular medication. He was bipolar. And he ran out of pills while we were in Costa Rica and had no easy way of getting more. Or he didn't try." Kelly talked slowly but lucidly. "I only found out afterward, although he was doing such totally weird stuff, I should have known."

"Like what?"

"Oh, Christ. Like he stopped brushing his teeth. Got into bar fights. Almost beat up a woman. Wore sunglasses at night and talked like he was a movie producer or something. I think it was an experiment. He wanted to see what would happen."

"Jesus. Why does this shit happen to you?"

"It doesn't. It happened to people I loved. I've always been drawn to big personalities, big appetites. The flip side of those things is sometimes tragic."

"You got it all figured out, kid."

"Yeah. That's why I'm broke, driving a borrowed car, and living in a closet."

I leaned against the wall, afraid to lie next to him. I scanned the cinder blocks. Shelves had been removed, leaving outlines of rust. Above us, one long industrial fluorescent light.

Library books on the floor: *The Tibetan Book of the Dead*, *Walden*, *The Ginger Man*. Neither of us spoke for a while.

"What's the best thing you've ever done?" I asked finally.

"I haven't done it yet," he answered.

"That's cheating."

"It won't be big or dramatic," he hurried to add. "I don't mean to say that. But it's on the horizon. I look forward to it."

"How can you live in here?"

"Oh, man," he said, sitting up. "I shower at the Y."

"But, I mean—"

"I know what you mean," he said. "To be honest, this is about all I can handle right now."

A blond beehived woman with ample bosom glared through bifocals. "Where you been, Lee."

"Hey, Doris."

We were back in Brooklyn. As a coda to our long and serpentine day, we'd decided after dropping off Angel to bring burritos from the taqueria over to Rosemary's Tavern. Androgynous kids shuffled by the jukebox, skunk stripes bleached down their heads, sheer vintage blouses showing nipples, tattoos. Polish men hunkered in booths, dressed in midnight-blue work clothes, grease under fingernails. The place was yellow with smoke.

"Guy scares me. I didn't like him."

"He intimidates you. He's obsessed with what he does. He does exactly what he loves, he works like an animal, and he's earned his independence. Everyone is jealous of him, don't worry."

"His independence from what?"

Kelly shrugged. "From everything."

I asked Kelly to tell me stories. He told me about bribing policemen in Costa Rican woods after getting caught buying cocaine. Skateboarding in an abandoned hotel pool in Jamaica, breaking his arm. Windsurfing on ice, on a board with steel runners. Untangling a dying hawk from a fence.

"I don't know," he said, suddenly shy. "All those places seem faraway now. Those stories sound like . . . I don't know. That's the kind of stuff you write on postcards."

"What do you mean?" I asked, sipping my Styrofoam cup of Bud.

He shrugged, smiled. "The stuff that changes your life is never very dramatic. You know? Not to other people."

"Yeah, I hear you. So tell me one of those stories."

"I don't know if I can. They're not really stories. They're just moments."

"Try."

"Okay," he said, licking beer foam from his lip. "One day, a couple years ago, before anything bad had happened, I was surfing. And I scraped my hand on coral. It slit me like a knife, but not deep. It was a bright day, the sun was blinding. It made the blood this fierce red against the blue water. I stood in the shallows and watched my hand bleed. I must have looked like a madman, you know, staring. But I couldn't stop."

I didn't say anything.

"It wasn't an omen," he added.

I looked at him.

"But it was something close to an omen," he said.

◇◇◇◇◇

We parted after last call. I stopped into a deli, watched him through the window. He walked down the street, easy as a beachcomber, keys glittering from his dark hand.

It wasn't a swagger or a skulk. He had a slow way of moving forward that paid homage to what was left behind, and to what was immediately around him, as well as to his destination.

He paused to read a wall of flyers.

He resumed walking. Fading into the ratty shearlings and moonlit faces and iron railings. He brought so much with him to this Brooklyn avenue, he kept so many things alive, but they didn't weigh him down. They didn't make him struggle. In fact, he wore them like a halo, a crown of phantom coconuts, conch shells, hibiscus blossoms.

A few nights later, I sat at my kitchen table, sketched in a book while coffee brewed.

"What do you think, Angel?" I said every once in a while, chewing my pencil.

I'd talked with an elderly man that day. He'd been walking with a cane, a ruby signet ring glinting on his finger. In the summer, he perused the sidewalks with shirtsleeves rolled, and I'd seen concentration-camp numbers on his arm. Big orange freckles covered his face. He had a sensual, rolling walk, even though he limped.

I put down the graphite pencil, closed my eyes. Soon I was on hands and knees, yanking fishnets across the dirty floor. Angel pounced. My Chanel N° 5 had rubbed onto her fur, and I scooped her up and pressed my cheek against hers. Maybe I would put on a record and lie in bed with Angel to think.

A cold and quick fever pricked my skin: a sensation explained to me when I was little as someone walking over my grave. Oh,

I knew this country. It was a bad place. This was where I went to let an endeavor subside. It was the halfway zone. I sat back on my heels, let Angel have the stockings. Lying on her side, she curled around them like a potato bug, biting the thread, clawing them with back paws.

I sat down at the table, chewed the pencil. The man. What did I know about him? I didn't know his name. Both his face and his gait reminded me of a younger man. Mainly his walk, slack with a bounce, studly. What had he said to me?

He'd raised his cane, gazed at it theatrically: "This here's my girlfriend."

I'd laughed for him.

"Don't get old," he said in an accent, tough and gentlemanly. "Getting old is the pits. I wouldn't wish it on a dog."

But the big grin contradicted what he told me. Contradicted it sternly enough to alert me to some other truth he was trying to tell me. It was late afternoon when we met. Snowflakes fell, early, errant ones that melted before they hit the sidewalk. Practice snowflakes. They were almost imaginary.

He'd worn a herringbone cap, softened but still in good form. He had looked up into the sky, and then at me. He was smiling at the snowflakes, articles of innocence, that fell from a dark sky.

Hours passed. The canvas on the easel was alive, breathing, blood running through its veins. The sky and the snowflakes and the man's freckled face were primitively rendered, and joined like the broken pieces of a teacup. In the looming dimensions and shadows resided the darkness of adult truths as well as the candy of children's dreams. The yellow beam from the streetlamp, the gleam of his cane were leaden as Freudian symbols, but the snow was spun sugar. Much work remained for tomorrow, and the next day, but so far the painting was greater than what I'd imagined. And that was the hallmark of a breakthrough. That's what I'd been awaiting.

"Motherfucking hell," I said loudly.

I strutted around. Picked up my hairbrush, combed once, threw it on the bed. Sat in the unlit room. A safety pin glittered on the bedside table. A chipped glass with an inch of milk glowed. Even in the darkness, everything burned with light. My fingernails, Angel's eyes.

Walked through dawn streets, hands in pockets. Nowhere to go. No one out here, no one at all, no wind, even. Just a still, dark mist enclosing railings, stoops, trees, garbage cans, broken toys on the curb, cars parked bumper to bumper, a shopping cart.

My God, charging up the middle of the street: a pit bull, his hide the color of vanilla ice cream, his face grotesque. But I wasn't scared. I stopped as he got closer. He slowed to sniff my pockets. And he wasn't lost. He ran down the street, right to a first-floor apartment, and in he jumped. From my angle, it seemed he leaped through the wall of the building. But there was a screech as the sleepy master pulled down the window.

Thanksgiving afternoon: the sky as blue as Caribbean water, but cold as ice.

I ran my hands over the dried paint, but it didn't make me as giddy. The design and the potential still thrilled me, but not as much. I didn't even want to go anywhere; I just wanted to work. That's when I realized that I could never stop. Because each little bit only kicks your heart like a can down one measure of the road. I remembered this passion as though the last time I'd felt it had been a thousand years ago: art begets art.

Overheated subway station, a sense of sparseness and irregularity due to the holiday. A man stood against a wall as if thrown there by an explosion; his feet were bare, scarred, one covering the other like feet nailed to a cross.

On the bench, a teenaged boy peeled a banana. I looked at the white spear, the petals of yellow. Its perfume was staggering, and flooded the whole station.

I jotted words on my hand.

Coming up from the subway in Manhattan, I thought it was raining on the steps above me. But no, it was a man pissing down the stairs. His penis and hands silver in lamplight.

"Happy Thanksgiving, motherfucker," I shouted up to him.

Instead of using the front door, I sneaked in Yves's kitchen door like a thief. The Raoul's boys were cooking dinner. Hand-rolled cigarettes burning on the sill.

Gifts out on the foyer table: red wine, plum lilies, soap in wax paper, a tin of foie gras. Everyone but me had brought something. I'd brought the black hole of my misfit personality: light fell into me. I spent much of the time bent over the cheese plate, hands clasped behind me, avoiding conversation.

His guests moved around like characters in the opening scene of a play.

"Muscadet?" Anson asked, handing me a glass of green wine, his thumb firmly grasping the base. His eyes twinkled when I smiled my thanks. A mustard cashmere sweater tied around his shoulders.

And I thought, these people would have a better time without me. I'd come late, as usual. Sashayed around in my black pencil skirt like a drunk starlet. Remembered almost no one's name, although they all knew mine. And up till now, I'd always thought they were pretty lucky to have me around. But I brought nothing but conspicuous silence.

Cranberry sauce crumbled in wet chunks as I spooned it to my plate.

Yves sat at the other head of the table and tried to catch my eye. When he did, I smiled wanly at him. Everyone was pink-cheeked, even the men, competing to put two cents into the conversation and trying to include me.

"You've been to Venice, haven't you, Lee?" someone asked.

"It's a knitwear boutique in Stockholm," someone else said. "Lee, you must know her stuff."

"Which is not the same as what happened in the beginning in Bosnia, don't you agree, Lee?"

I answered yes to everything. Sure, I'd been to Venice. Why not? I could feel Yves, at the opposite end of the table, trying hard not to hear my lies, but becoming concerned.

"Excuse me, Delphine," I said, patting my mouth with my napkin. I turned to Anson, on my other side. "Excuse me." Yves's eyes followed me to the kitchen, but he didn't get up.

The boys stared at a travel backgammon set between them. So engrossed in their game, they didn't look when I whispered good-bye.

My cheeks flamed when I walked into the warm studio. Kelly, in jeans and shetland sweater, wore five-o'clock shadow. Football played on a black-and-white TV, a Guinness on the floor next to a folding chair.

"I'm sorry," I whispered.

"For what," he whispered back, making fun of me.

I tried to make a joke, but blundered. We both realized I was extraordinarily drunk.

I tried to explain the foie gras and the lilies, my empty hands, the back door. As I spoke, his eyes deepened, his mouth grew wary.

"So you didn't tell anyone you were leaving?" he said. "You didn't tell Yves?"

"Well," I said, gesturing. "No."

"So you just left him to explain your disappearance to a table of his close friends. On Thanksgiving."

I looked steadily at him, but he looked steadily at me. So I started crying. I expected Kelly to grab a tissue, but he didn't.

"Fuck," I wailed. "I just want it to be over."

"And?" he said, on the brink of disgust.

"Christ," I said raspily, "I don't want to think about any of this."

He seemed to be framing a thought the way he pursed his lips, clasped his hands. Instead, he repeated what I'd said: "You don't want to think about any of this."

"You have a problem with that."

He nodded. "I do."

"I thought you liked ladies in distress."

Looking at the floor, he paused before he said quietly: "Come on, Lee. Nick cleans houses for a living, pays her bills, and listens to records. She never asked for help. If anything, she could do without my help and humors me because that's who she is."

He glared at me with disappointment. I saw, then, in his eyes, some hopeful vision turn to a lifetime of nights like this one, but with sun blazing outside, or a different cityscape blinking, or us wearing different clothes, using different words. Shattered nights, scattered talks—but nothing that would amount to more than a wet sleeve, midnight prayers and contracts and resolutions, morning-time disenchantment, empty bottles, sticky glasses, stinking ashtrays.

He stood up, with effort.

"Lee," he said finally, "I am just not interested in taking care of you. I am very sorry if I gave you the impression that I was."

And he walked into the hallway. Held the door open for me, his head bowed as I exited.

When I got home, I dialed half his number. Maybe he regretted what he'd said and would apologize. No, *you bimbo*, I thought to myself. The kid wasn't sorry. And he wasn't going to come out here, no matter how much I begged. He probably wouldn't even answer my call.

So I took off my clothes. Scrubbed my body in a hot shower for a long time. Stared into the mirror at the pale face, red eyes, stringy hair until I was able to operate my features. In a kimono, hair dripping, I brewed coffee. I couldn't think right, my thoughts lurching from one place to another.

Swallowed the coffee black. In the sink, I ran cold water on face, wrists. Slapped my cheek.

"Okay, sweet thing," I said. "Focus, for fuck's sake."

Turning on all overhead lights was spooky, as if a tunnel of caves was illuminated for the first time. My nerves were electric. A hangover was coming on in degrees.

I moved from kitchen to bedroom, from cupboard to drawer, from Levi's pockets to leopard clutch. I tore things up. Angel loved it, chasing after my silk belt.

Opera on the radio. Incense.

In between, I bent to the sink and gulped water from my hands.

I thought of mobster movies, but there was no policeman at

my door. Just the past, with his own nightstick. My reflection swept by in the mirror, red hair flying, black sleeves flapping, but I couldn't stop to think what I was doing. I'd compulsively hoarded, as if sandbagging a foxhole. Newport Kings in the freezer. A bag of coke in my underwear drawer. The drugs went in the toilet, the liquor down the sink. Took the garbage bag of bottles and cans to the curb, pulling kimono lapels tight.

I never went to bed sober, but here I was. The energy used up, the liquor passed through the body, the desires exhausted. Sleep had always been my way station, a hiding place where the night's events could fade without contemplation. Not that I was sure now for whom I'd done this, or how I would deal with the morning. But I was spent, and conscious. I'd gone past the place where I usually surrendered and had traveled into unknown territory.

Lying in the sheets, Angel curled against my stomach, I said: "It's just you and me, babydoll."

My apartment is bare, I thought dreamily as we drifted.

My mother and I skinny-dipped when the Blackmans were out of town. Standing in the shallow end, our torsos wet with moonlight, legs shining underwater. I bounced on tiptoes, too ecstatic to be still. Skin ablaze with night. Unable to contain joy, we pushed forward, like geese landing. Sent up wakes of sparks and feathers. Oh, the glamour of nothing. Bare skin and flat hair and dark faces and our own rain.

Afterward, we ran screeching home in towels as if fleeing a crime. We squealed past rhododendrons, our pink-gowned chaperones, that trembled in midnight heat. The whole scene was preserved, like a snow globe. I could still shake it, watch stars collide.

<><><><>

A few days later, after Kelly and I worked an excruciatingly awkward brunch together, I lured him into talking to me. I had a theory. I had a strategy. I'd suggested we go somewhere, offered to take him to dinner that night. Used the fact that we'd have to work together too often to be at odds.

"Naw," he'd said, not looking at me. "Let's just go sit outside somewhere."

We walked without talking across the West Side Highway and down along the Hudson to a bench that faced the river. When he finally turned to me, his face showed a combination of exasperation and pity. I almost gave up before I began.

"I'm not going to ask you for help," I said quickly, voice small.

I cleared my throat, knowing nothing was as damaging as uncertainty.

"I was hoping I could ask you a few questions," I continued. "That's all."

He rolled his eyes. "Lee, it's not even that I don't want to help you. I *can't*. I cannot give you what you need."

"What if," I rushed on, "you just let me ask about the way you live. I won't ask for advice. And this will be a better end to things than what happened."

He said he just didn't want to get into anything more, but almost had to suppress a smile, as if intrigued by being interviewed.

This made me sure enough to say: "Come on, Kelly. It won't hurt. Deal?"

Even though he shook his head, he said: "Deal."

The day's cold was heavy and humid, and the water gray. But the sun flickered now to make a white sparkle on the waves and then turned the expanse to pounded gold. He took off his sweater, then had to pull down the black long-john shirt he wore over his button-down.

"So, what are your questions," he said.

"So," I started, clearing my throat again, "what do you really want?"

"We went over this already," he said blandly.

"Well, you told me you wanted to restructure your life, that you wanted to start over and all that. You found Nick—" I barely spoke her name, so embarrassed about the way I'd brought her up before. "And all that, but I still don't know exactly what you want."

"To make every hour matter."

"And you think you can do that?"

"I know I can do that."

I looked at the lipstick marks on my coffee lid. "How are you going to do that?" I whispered.

"We're not in church, Lee," he said sardonically.

Then he looked at the sky, and back at me. "I'm dismantling my life. It's in pieces as we speak." His hands were laced around one knee, pulling up the leg so the foot didn't touch the ground.

"And you do that how, exactly?"

"Well. I don't know how to explain this. Let's see. I was reading about this guy who saved an organ from a church that was being torn down. He didn't know shit about organs, really, or any instrument, but he flatbedded it to his garage. Where there was a screw, he unscrewed. He put numbers on everything—every pipe, every pedal. Found someone to make new reeds. Then he reassembled it in his barn, and when it was done, he somehow could play songs.

"I didn't used to work. I thought I lived the life. Made money in surf contests. We knew all the judges; they knew us. Me and my friends buddied up to rich tourists. I drank on other people's tabs. I'd get in on the occasional drug deal. I don't know. My friends and I even ripped each other off. I was in jail once—"

I raised my eyebrows.

"Nothing big, a fight. I told Greg where to find my cash to bail me out; he took it and went on a three-day binge with two other guys. Kind of funny. I always told it like it was a funny story."

"It is kind of funny," I said.

"Enough out of you," he said. Then he sighed. "So. For a while, I knew it wasn't right—"

"What?"

"My life."

"Don't tell me you found Jesus."

"No." He snorted. "No. But I knew, even before that happened to Nick, I had to get it together. But I didn't know how to fix it because I didn't know how it was made. So I decided to break down my time by year, by week, by hour. Figure out how I was spending my life. What I ate, drank, loved, made, hurt, saw, learned. Bought. Stole. Gave."

"That sounds impossible."

"It's the easiest thing in the world." He pointed to the notebook on the bench beside him, tattered pages bulging.

I asked to see it.

"Absolutely not," he said.

We were quiet for a moment. On the other benches, suits sat in winter reveries.

I thought of something. "But you did work. You were a bartender," I said.

"I never bartended. I just memorized a cocktail book."

"You can't learn bartending from a book."

"Yes, you can," he said simply, without argument. "I never knew how to first mate either, but I knew how to fish, and I needed a ride."

"What else have you been up to?"

He scanned the opposite shore, then reddened. He grinned, the first time all afternoon he'd shown his teeth. The wind was light, made his hair tremble. He admitted that the night before he'd made cookies. *From scratch*, he said twice, as if I'd argued.

"I can't believe you baked cookies, Kelly. I mean that," I said, "in the best possible way."

"I know," he said. "It's fucked-up. But now I want to bake a cake. I'm hooked. I even wear an apron, you know. The whole nine yards, Lee."

"Is it coming together then?" I asked after a while.

"Hell no," he said emphatically, knowing what I meant. Then yawned, making his face pink, eyes watery. "Hell no," he said quietly, but not sadly. "Still mainly coming apart, I guess."

The picture of Kelly in an apron, powder on his cheek, sifter in hand, almost broke my heart. He was like an alien enchanted by life on Earth, so enamored he was willing to try.

For a moment I was tempted to tell him about what I'd done, what I was trying to do. But my whole life I'd been working from the template of love being sloppy. A big martini sloshing over the sides of the glass. Maybe strength and reserve would serve us better. Kelly had proved during the conversation by the choice of a word here and an intonation there that he'd love me if I didn't make it impossible. Which is what I'd been doing. He reminded me of a deer: powerful, lightning fast, and autonomous, but delicate and curious. In a way, stillness was my best chance.

"Thanks," I said, and although he looked surprised that the interview was over, we stood.

In the distance, violet clouds weighed heavily on the Jersey skyline. We left behind a man who'd been standing at the rail when we sat down, and was still doing so, and looked as if he might forever. A messenger bag strapped across his back, the wires of earphones attached to the Discman in his hand. His raven-black hair ruffled like feathers by the breeze. He was a figurehead at the bow of Manhattan.

◇◇◇◇◇

Jeremy took me to dinner at Paul and Frank's house a few times during my first year on the Cape. They lived at the end of a long dirt road so overgrown that branches snapped against Jeremy's ancient Datsun as we crawled over the ruts. Their home was like a huge shed, with arbitrary porches and crazy angles, vines of blue clematis blazing up the wood shingles in the dusk.

Their chickens were fed on rosemary and table scraps and top-notch grains. The eggs' yolks were so orange that the coconut cakes Paul baked weren't white. Half-wild cats chased baby bunnies through the gardens, and citronella candles burned yellow in buckets on the edges of the patio. The bed was a box spring and mattress on cinder blocks shrouded in mosquito netting. They had a piano someone had painted red, its ivory keys dark as bad teeth.

We'd sit in lawn chairs and laugh in the quiet way required of easy, supernatural evenings. The lake wasn't far, but it wasn't visible except as a shimmer through dense trees. They were both in their late thirties. Paul had worked as an accountant in Boston for years and had saved enough that neither of them had to work anymore. They weren't artists, and they weren't bitter recluses. They were simply deliberate. Nothing they did required more than a bike ride. Two bikes slanted against the house in all weather, one pink, the other white, rust stains dripping like blood down their parts.

Paul and Frank communicated without words. They looked at each other for a long moment, and then one announced their decision. They never preached about how to live, but I knew they could instruct me if I asked. I thought about asking once. In a blue woody light, we sipped homemade sangria full of jewel-sized homegrown strawberries. I knew they were waiting for me to speak my mind. But I wasn't ready then to hear what they would say.

SEVEN

◇◇◇◇

I have just realized that the stakes are myself
I have no other
ransom money, nothing to break or barter but my life
my spirit measured out, in bits, spread over
the roulette table, I recoup what I can
nothing else to shove under the nose of the maitre de jeu

—DIANE DI PRIMA, from *Revolutionary Letters*

unch at the restaurant a couple days later was winter weekend madness. Mirrors sparkled, gold stools winked. Kelly's black necktie was stitched with a stranger's cursive white monogram. We passed looks with straight expressions because we didn't know what the other was thinking. Myself, I swung between two pinnacles every twenty seconds. First I was ready to take a tire iron to the windows, mirrors, glasses, bottles. Then I'd find myself high on sobriety, smiling dazedly at everyone with clarity and nebulous gratitude. My headache, I'd later learn, was because of withdrawal from, of all things, caffeine.

None of the staff knew what I was doing. They were suspicious of the jasmine teas and club sodas with bitters I asked them to make me, but no one said anything. Each time I passed Kelly, I smiled professionally, didn't allow the moment to linger long enough for him to ask or me to confess.

One table knocked back Absolut Peppar bloody Marys. Glassy-eyed in the daytime. I tried to look down on them with all my heart. Here they were, throwing this day away, tossing it to the gods as if it were a virgin. They giggled. They ordered a banana split to share. They showed no sign of leaving. I believed they were my enemies.

At four o'clock, I had a minute alone as I was clocking out, and I folded. I had been putting on my coat in the office, pulling the gloves out of pockets, and I just stopped what I was doing. Stood still as a statue.

"Cold turkey," Kelly said behind me, and I jumped.

"I am pathetically obvious," I answered, unable to look at him.

"Damn, girl," he drawled. "That's excellent."

I sat heavily on the chair, one glove on, one off. "Yeah, but I wasn't going to tell you because I'm not even going to make it through the day." I shot him a lopsided grin. "I mean, what's TV without smokes? What's sushi without beer? What's the movies without a joint?"

"So you can't go to the movies and get popcorn."

"No. I can get high and go to the movies and get popcorn. It's the difference between being in love or not." Suddenly I looked at him in fear. "I'm not asking you for help, by the way. That's not what I'm doing."

He laughed, pulled a pom-pom hat over his head. "I know. It's okay."

"Oh, hell." I gazed at my boots. "There's just nothing as tacky as being on the wagon."

Kelly suggested he walk me home.

"I walk over to Seventh," I said. "I get the One-Nine."

"No, I mean, walk you home."

"Kelly Bradley." I grabbed him by the biceps and spoke clearly. "I live in Brooklyn. Home is in Brooklyn."

"I know. Let's walk. It will give you something to do."

The river's motion was invisible, but water rushed barges under the bridge.

We stepped over graffiti written on the asphalt path. A long poem in German. A portrait of a schoolboy with his cock out, pissing, cigarette between lips. Scrawled: *Criminalize Wealth. Landlords evict spies.* And *Good night Juanita.* On the edge of the walkway: junkie vomit, pigeon feathers. The smell of almost-burned sugar in the sky.

Matte-gray girders divided pearly clouds. On the Brooklyn side, what was closest to us was lucid, like the red neon Domino sugar factory sign, but beyond was veiled by a layer of plum silk.

When I took the train, I never acknowledged this passage. I went underground, I came up later, like a prairie dog. But crossing the water, with pale-blue Manhattan behind us, and maroon-and-mustard Brooklyn ahead, I understood that I lived in a town, firmly planted on land. Before this, Brooklyn had seemed a figment of many imaginations, a place solely made from the words and deeds of many generations.

Even when Kelly hunched into his jacket against the wind, his face was turned to the sun. Just a California boy on a New York winter day, walking a girl home. The blond fur tufts from his hood, framing his face, reminded me of sunflower petals.

On Bedford, we came upon a church sale. A garment rack was being pulled inside by a huge woman in a baby-blue coat. Her hat with black poppies was one degree of purple less black than her skin. Left on the sidewalk: record albums. A small library of songs no one wanted to hear anymore.

As Kelly squatted, the woman came back outside, and I pointed out to him that she was closing up.

"No," the woman said with an island accent, smiling but looking down the street, pulling her coat's lapels, kind and dissociated at the same time. "Lookit 'um. Go head."

He scanned titles quickly, flipping through jackets. I saw the boy he might have been, standing in a stationery store reading BMX magazines, comic books, tattoo trades.

My apartment smelled as if an invalid had been sleeping there. Drawings in a pile on the kitchen table were paperweighted by a sticky jar of honey.

"How's my girl." He scratched Angel's head.

She mewed as I collected lingerie and junk mail.

We'd bought books from the one-dollar shelves of a bookstore. Then he'd gotten the makings of Mexican hot chocolate at a deli. He managed to use three pots, a couple knives, and a few spoons. Left chocolate shavings on the counter, cinnamon and burned milk on the stove. The sun had vanished, and he cooked in the dark. The only light was the violet blossom of gas flame.

Settled into my stereo room on big pillows. The chocolate tasted like a lullaby. When I asked how he knew the recipe, Kelly said his mother was Mexican. Why had he never told me? He rolled his eyes. I'd never asked.

The ten-record set was called Background Moods. Each side, a different mood. The green box featured a kohl-eyed woman with pale pink lips, a sweep of dark hair across her forehead, and a rainy window in between us and her.

"Oh, this is brilliant," I said, pulling out one record. "I have to hear *In an Exotic Mood*. I want to hear song number five, 'Beyond the Blue Horizon.'"

It started with small plucks of music and crept into something vaguely Hawaiian. I grinned, sipping my chocolate.

"I think I hear some harp," Kelly said doubtfully.

Standing at the door in his parka, paperback in his pocket, he seemed uncertain. I asked if he wanted his records. He said he guessed he'd leave them.

"Is that a gift?" I asked. "Are you giving me a present?"

He shrugged, and by the flavor of the movement, I realized in a flash what had been evident all along.

"How old are you?" I asked.

"Twenty-nine."

"You've never been in love," I said softly.

He started to protest.

"You've never had a girlfriend."

"I've had many girlfriends."

"I mean, you've never had a proper girlfriend."

Once more, he shrugged. Pecked me on the cheek and jumped down the stairs two steps at a time like a teenager.

It was eleven that night by the time I got over there. I'd been avoiding Yves with dubious excuses, and he'd become guarded, even cold. He hadn't let the tension come to a head, so I would have to do the dirty work. I woke Yves out of bed. The loft was dark, and I asked him to leave it dark.

He hugged me, past the right moment for letting go. And my skeleton started to melt, like it did that first time, releasing fears and shames, giving itself away.

But I didn't want that, and struggled. He gave a last squeeze, the way parents do when they don't want you to disappoint them.

We sat in his living room, in a darkness that betrayed forms but not colors. The gloom sealed the room, its furniture, its corners, its windows, and its owner, bonded them so I would remember the space as one piece.

He started talking, running his sentences together so there was no place for me to break into the discussion. He kept repeating that there were a lot of things for us to hash out, to get through. He spoke with hands on arms of chair like Lincoln.

I went deaf looking at his silhouette, topped by the shimmer of his hair, still but for a flash of tooth. I no longer saw a king presiding over possibilities, but an ordinary man working his fingers to the bone to maintain the idea of possibilities.

After a while, I went over and pressed the ring into his hand. He stopped talking.

Rain struck the window. I walked to the door.

"I'm going to pay you back," I said, turning around, my hand on the doorknob.

"Pay me back what?" he asked, incredulous.

"The money. All the money."

"That is an insult, Lee," he said evenly and urgently.

My face wanted to crumble, and I fought to keep it straight. "I have to. I'm so sorry—"

"An insult."

"I don't want to owe you," I said, tears welling, aware I was saying the wrong things. "I mean—"

"Oh, for Christ's sake," he said, hands on hips, turning away.

"I'm sorry," I said again.

"Just go home, Lee," he said, sounding so tired, still looking away.

As he heard me turn the knob, he looked at me. "Wait," he said, and picked an umbrella from the stand. Black silk, ivory handle.

"No, Yves. I don't want it."

"It's raining," he said.

"I don't want it," I said in a shrill voice.

His face crimson, eyes absurdly wide. He spit when he yelled. "You don't want my umbrella?" His accent swelled, voice thick and dense. "You don't want it?"

He hurled it into the living room; it smashed the white lamp, which fell to the floor in sparks that died quickly.

I stood, shaking, on the other side of the door.

I pictured him wandering his loft tomorrow, dressed properly, picking up and putting down the odds and ends of existence—a half-melted drink, the newspaper, his reading glasses—aimlessly pursuing or evading something he couldn't see.

Was I so vain to think I'd done him in? Wrecked him? Did I think that Yves was even damaged? Was he anything besides pissed, disgruntled, disconcerted, his tie askew, cufflink lost on floor, glasses bent? All he had to do was brush himself off, clear his throat, and comb his hair.

Had he loved me, or did I just keep him from feeling old, or lonely, or mortal? The only thing I knew for sure as I pulled my jacket around my face to brave that rain was that now he hated me.

A few nights after, Kelly wanted me to have dinner with him and Guy, but I'd have been bad company. Sherry called about a party for a guy named Jesse. It seemed like a good idea: I'd get out of the house but wouldn't see many people I knew. I went alone, scuffing through icy litter on the Southside. The foyer was propped open, and the bulb illuminated crooked stairs.

I could test myself. Already my days had doubled in length, my strength had tripled, but sobriety was excruciating every minute. My instinct was to stay home forever, but that was a cop-out. It hadn't been a substance problem; the substances were symptoms of a bigger failing. Vodka and cigarettes had become shortcuts, and the muscles I'd used as a child atrophied. The defect was a laziness, an unwillingness to do the hard labor of living.

One repercussion was the appetites I'd created, empty places that could only be filled in particular ways. Nothing warms the torso exactly like brandy. Nothing swells the lungs like smoke. I wasn't born wanting cocaine's numb front teeth, but I'd built that fetish from experience. I imagined my heart as a chunk of coral: tunneled, calcified.

What can I say? It was like most parties. Boys and girls. Cake.

A kid in the corner wearing a leather beret, playing synthesizer. Christmas lights rocked back and forth, casting shadows as people stomped on the floor.

Jesse was stunning. Jug-eared and bowlegged in a black denim jacket, with a birthday high that made me jealous. In one hand, whiskey in a plastic cup, in the other, a beer bottle, a joint hanging from his lips, eyes slit.

The bad feeling escalated when girls broke out bottles of cheap champagne.

"No, thanks," I said, shielding my mouth.

"C'mon," one said.

"No, no," I said, thinking that I was in a bad after-school special.

"A li'l can't hurt," she slurred, and in the end, spilled it down my shirt.

"Sorry." She hiccuped.

In the kitchen, I dabbed at the wetness. I couldn't do this. I couldn't stand to be here. I didn't know who I was. But I refused to leave, to solidify my defeat. I stood guard in the living room, sipping orange juice, like a cop.

Early in the morning, with only a small crew left, Sherry came out of the bedroom in her own birthday suit. Standing like a queen, eating cake from a plate she held aloft, she was met first by silence, then applause. White sandals glowed on her black feet. Her long limbs gleamed under the strings of lights. A violet thatch between her thighs.

Praise the lord. I would always love the beautiful things that happen at night.

Walked home, hands crammed into pockets, breath rolling out.

A birdcage on the curb with bundled newspapers, its bars

shiny with ice. With wheelchairs, too, it was possible to imagine two scenarios. I hoped the bird got a better cage.

Me, lying in sheets, morning snowflakes turning like wagon wheels in the Brooklyn sky, Angel purring, phone pressed to my cheek. Art, in his green parlor out east, bifocals pushed up, slippers, Stanley Turrentine on the record player, Becca alighting on one arm of his chair then the other like a moth. She must have been concerned that he tell me in the kindest way, and probably mouthed words to him, maybe reached for the phone. I think he expected me to cry. And I should have cried.

I'd called to tell him to put the house on the market, but he had news of his own. My mother hadn't owned the house. She hadn't even paid rent. After living there for years, my mother gave Art my college money when it became obvious I wouldn't need it. It was a vague down payment, as if she could ever afford the balance.

"But that's the most absurd thing I've ever heard," I said. "She must have known I had to find out one day."

"Yes," Art said slowly, still waiting for me to break down.

"That's just crazy," I said, laughing. "That's totally insane."

Silence on the other end. I imagined Art shrugging at his wife, trying to indicate that I was fine. I thought of the looks they'd exchanged when I had lunch with them. I told Art he could have told me earlier.

"I wanted you to feel the house was yours."

"Now you sound as crazy as my mother," I scolded.

He sighed. "Ginger had a way of, how should I say, drawing a person in. It never seemed crazy the way she explained it. Part of why we loved her."

Maybe I wasn't surprised because I'd known all along. This

strange inheritance of good intentions and nothing else was in much better keeping with my mother's spirit. Art wasn't the enemy. He didn't care about property value more than he cared about me; in fact, it was the other way around. We talked over the options, until I convinced him I had only one option, meaning there actually weren't options at all. I was grateful for what he offered as a return of my mother's "original investment," knowing it was more than I was owed.

I accepted, knowing it was less than I owed Yves.

"Tell her to come out for eggnog and gingersnaps, Art," I heard Becca say. "Tell her."

During our life together, my mom and I were each other's houseguest. That's not to say we were always standoffish and too polite: there were pillow fights and duels of silence and decadent rainy-day sessions of dress-up. But it means we always gave each other room. We had to because it was only the two of us, and if we hadn't, we would have become one person. It means we kept secrets from each other. She didn't tell me how to live, and I didn't tell her how to die. We let sleeping dogs lie.

My father had reminded me of a gorilla: more human than humans, but not human at all. His beard stank, a filter for his bad breath. On one of his rare visits, we walked in woods that were blue with the prospect of rain. For his every stride, I skipped three times. I finally confessed to not knowing what kindling, which we were supposed to be collecting, was.

"The little ones," he'd said, "that get the big ones burning."

Echoes of genius or importance: whatever poem he was memorizing written on a scroll and tucked into his hatband, a smokehouse blueprint sketched on the wall by the toilet, a fly tied one

Christmas dinner with tinsel, an ornament hook, and a fur tuft from my jacket.

When he stayed with us, it was less as the man of the family and more as an art fellow, a visiting lecturer.

His career as an architect lasted ten years, and Art introduced him to my mother at the end of those years, before that end was evident. He'd burned bright. And then he was done. When the relationship began, he'd been working on a museum in Denmark, and everyone involved believed the building would be a groundbreaking and historical monument. By the time my mother fell in love and conceived me, the building was millions over budget, and my father was known internationally as a man who was failing, who was going down. His brilliance had been tied to a narcissism that allowed him to believe he could create anything he imagined. But his disdain for reality couldn't support his dreams. He'd become Unhappy. He died of Exhaustion. He left us Some Money.

I'd always suspected that his mammoth black beard, whose gray was as delineated as streaks of paint, had strangled him. I'd believed my mother refused to marry because she was a free spirit. I'd assumed we owned the house we lived in. I'd always trusted that our little world was safe because we deserved safety, not because she worked hard to make a nest for us. I'd been convinced that my mother recovered from losing him. But these were the activities of my mind. My heart perceived wildernesses of contradictions and impossible truths and mystical lies.

My mom worked at an antique store in East Hampton, a job I'd thought she did to keep from being bored. A dish of peppermints sat next to a calculator on the French pine table where she sat. In the drawer, money was filed big to small in a white envelope. A black Westie, whose hair was oily and plastered to its stout body, lay coiled in a basket and farted all day. I played with dolls on the kilims in the bitter fragrance of wood and rug. Sometimes I sat under the table, in the company of her freckled legs. We were warm and cozy, and we needed no one.

She divided her time between reading magazines; gossiping, hands on hips, with visitors; and arranging knickknacks and paintings. Once, she spent a day on two porcelain teacups. A peony branch had been painted on each one to grow from the exterior into the cup. After trying every corner of the shop, she settled them on a nightstand, exactly as if some dreamer in the middle of the night could actually reach out for a sip.

The Stinger Club. Bordello gloom throughout the place, and a back room where bad things happened. I once watched a wheel-chairbound man in gang colors, leg outstretched in a metal halo, crash around in the red dark, too drunk to drive his electric chair.

But tonight white boys were playing bluegrass. Kelly and I sat in a booth, shared a Coke with grenadine like a couple at a soda fountain. Something about the banjos: they promised that no matter how hard we'd worked, someone else had worked harder, and if he could let go, we should, too.

Kelly knew by the way I held his hand. He knew by the weight of my head on his shoulder. I never had to say a word. When the band broke, the players dropped their instruments on the stage to get beers, like kids abruptly abandoning toys for candy, and Kelly led me out. He walked me home as if I was a sleepwalker, as if it would be dangerous to wake me.

We stood in my dark kitchen, the stove and walls and refrigerator and our bodies streaked by blue headlights. We stood in that classical pose: my back against the wall, one knee raised between his thighs. His forearm on the wall above my head, our foreheads touching so we could look down onto each other's lips.

I woke to French toast smoke. We shared a big plate in bed. He licked syrup from my fingers. Angel moved around, disrupted by our own movements but wanting our heat. She glared at us.

As he wiped bread crust on the plate, I found my way down to his knees. Embraced his thighs lazily with one arm, sucked him like a baby fallen asleep with a rattle in her mouth. My negligee stretched almost to ripping, threadbare as lace left in the rain.

Before he went to work one day, we walked to stretch our love-strained legs. At a ninety-nine-cent store, we bought gifts, exchanged them outside in the magnificent cold white light of that Brooklyn morning. He got Old Spice aftershave. I got a white polyester nightgown.

"Decadent," he said.

"Glamorous," I agreed.

While waiting for him to come home that evening, I made old-fashioned meat loaf. Like a new bride, I put on the nightie and with bare hands worked egg into the raw beef. Before I put it in the hot oven, I laid bacon strips over the loaf as gently as tucking a child into bed. My negligee held creases where it had been folded and smelled of store, but when Kelly came home, we would break it in, make it mine.

ooooo

I got up as early as he did now. Sometimes at midnight my words still slurred, out of physiological habit. And in the mornings, I woke with a hangover on occasion, before realizing that was impossible. Most days I got up famished because I was used to consuming thousands of calories in liquor a night. Some days I woke up burning with anger, and I walked it out, worked it out, yet there was nothing to do but burn. His kisses burned my back. The cold shower burned. The cool bedsheets burned. But every time I brushed my teeth and picked out clothes for the day, no matter what else was happening in my head, I was amazed to find no damage, no destruction to inventory. That blessing never ceased to be revolutionary.

Standing this morning at the window in my black kimono, hair tangled in a bun, I watched ladies in black lamb's wool and pink lipstick totter to church. A new town unfolded in these early hours, new to me. These women spent afternoons in house-dresses and curlers, hanging out their windows, talking across the street. I used to think they never left their apartments. I used to feel sorry for them.

I turned to Kelly, who lay in bed with arms behind his head. "Don't you love it here?" I asked.

He looked at me, and finally answered. This was how it all got started. The plan blossomed like a tropical flower, hot and fervent.

"I couldn't," I said, when I crawled back into bed.

"But you could."

I lay across his chest, face turned sideways on his sternum. Drunk on the musk of his armpits. "Where?" I asked.

"Anywhere."

I almost dozed off, but managed to say in a sleepy voice: "You knew from the beginning that this would happen."

But he didn't answer.

◇◇◇◇◇

He dragged me up the hallway ladder to a roof I'd never ex-
plored. He said he couldn't believe I'd never come up here. The
tar-paper surface was slightly slanted. The December night was
lush, impossible for snow. Giddy, we turned around, surrounded
by a planetarium of stars and city.

It wasn't too warm to pretend we were cold.

"Come here," he said, and we huddled against the cement-
filled chimney.

Somehow we opened our coats to each other, as if they were
wings, and nestled like turtledoves. I pulled down his zipper, he
pushed up my skirt. Like a tusk, it angled up, but he missed as
often as he scored. Somehow this made me want it more than I
ever had before.

One arm around his neck, I bit my own thumb. In the blindness of it all, he stumbled, knees locked by blue jeans. We laughed,
steadied ourselves, started again.

"Come on," I said, tremulous "Keep going."

Through my tears, I couldn't tell the stars from the skyline.

In the golden sun of the slow afternoon, Kelly cut limes. The
light turned the fruit to green crystal. A backward *S*, from the
restaurant's name painted on the window, was emblazoned on
his white shirt.

"It's a place for outsiders," Kelly said. "The resort of last resort."

I turned the pages of the book. White gingerbread porch,
gecko on the post like a mezuzah. A rooster like a small fire

under a larger fire of bougainvillea. Bikers eating Cuban sand-wiches at a café, tattoo of a peace sign on one's beefy shoulder.

"People like us," I said, and blushed.

Making this plan with him made me blush when it crossed my mind, even while I was alone. Such things are few and far between that turn our cheeks red by innocence, not lewdness.

The places we'd looked at online were crude, but not crude enough to be quaint. Linoleum, carport, plastic venetian blinds were what we could afford. But someone once said that luxury wasn't the opposite of poverty, but of vulgarity, and Kelly and I were planning a luxurious life. We would pay rent on time. File taxes, even. Vote. Volunteer. Recycle. We'd come home from work, toss dirty uniforms into washer, cook steaks on a Smokey Joe under an emerald evening sky, say our Florida prayers, and dream the dreams of good citizens.

We made love for a long, slow time in the pitch black, under the covers. At first, my mind retained his body, even though I couldn't see. I saw the ghost of him lying with me. The length of leg, the glowing curve of shoulder. Distended like a white doll in black water. We went deeper into each other, and my mind lost his body. What I got instead was bits of white petal and gold fur and red berry. This is what the heart sends up when you enter the dream part of loving. The soul wants visible company but finally lets go of the idea of two people. We kept moving, for hours. Maybe I was falling asleep, or maybe I was waking up. Now I could see his childhood, stretched out in farms and air-fields and church parking lots. Planes crossed blue skies above suburbs. I saw the skyline of all his nights. I heard his fights echo off barroom walls, heard sirens chase him down streets, felt turquoise waves crush and lift him. Now I strolled through a vineyard and came upon him with a black-haired girl. Two pairs of jeans folded in wet grass next to toppled wine coolers. A leather-tooled handbag leaned against the vines, wet with rain, rain falling from the leaves. The bag full of teenage-girl things: cherry lip gloss, gum, keys. A bit of blood on his cock when she got off, and he held it up as he waited for her to lie on her back, as they had silently, physically agreed to change positions. And they continued now with him on top. He was younger in this vineyard, but it didn't make me jealous to see his bony shoulders working, to hear him almost crying. Instead it made me proud to see her eyes turn back, the whites rolling. Because I had become the stars in the sky above them.

At the end of my shift, I went down to the office to put on Adidas sneakers, shoved shoes in a drawer. That's the way I did things now. I walked over the dusky bridge in my red coat as if communicating to God that I was alive. Kelly met me at Alioli. He asked if I was cold. I asked if he was hungry. We ate hot prawns at the bar with our cold fingers.

I told him his face reminded me of a figure from a totem pole. He said he'd seen a fire that day on the Lower East Side, but he thought the building was abandoned. I said that I was full. He said that he was sleepy.

At home he made hot chocolate, but tonight it tasted different. Too much nutmeg, he decided. He wore long-john bottoms to bed; I wore my dollar teddy. He'd heard it might snow tonight, as much as six inches. I said I wished it would, because I loved the quiet after. We couldn't sleep and stared together at the dark.

"We're moving to Florida, aren't we," I said.

"Yes," he said. "We are."

◇◇◇◇

All I had to give was two weeks' notice, which I'd do after New Year's. The staff was structured so anyone could be replaced. I paid January's rent, told Anthony I'd be out by February first. My lease was just a handshake, and he and I both knew I could leave when I wanted. I didn't want to say good-bye to friends. In the past year, we'd all grown apart, irrevocably. They'd started families or had simply forgotten me. I hoped to be missed but didn't expect it.

Almost every day I walked to or from work. When I woke, I felt strong and lucid. My appetite was ferocious, but my sweet tooth was gone. I craved meat, raw carrots, walnuts, yogurt.

Kelly brought me cardboard boxes from the bodega. Because I had to pack up both the apartment and then the house out east, the sooner I started, the better. My goal was to radically minimize. When I listed the things I would give away, even Kelly was surprised.

One day our plan changed. Kelly had made calls to Key West friends to find a pull-out couch where we could crash in February so that we could start looking for a place. His friend T.J. called him back. If Kelly went down immediately and helped renovate a unit T.J. owned, we could take possession February first and get the first month free as payment for the work.

Art had just wired me funds, and after I paid Yves half of what I owed him, I'd have ten grand left. I told Kelly he didn't need to do this work, that I could pay the first month. But he said it didn't feel right to him, and that this was a perfect solution. A month without him seemed like a horrible idea, but he was determined. We found him a ticket online for Christmas, four days away.

We tangoed in my kitchen, euphoric, scared, ridiculous.

I mailed Yves a certified check. I folded it in the last blank sheet of paper in the box. I'd used all the others trying to compose a letter, but there was nothing to say. Eventually I'd pay him in full. Since the funds were certified, they'd already been removed from my account. It didn't matter if Yves burned the check—the money could never come back to me. In a perverse way, it would be funny if he never deposited the check. Thirty-eight grand would float in a purgatory of bank transactions.

Christmas Eve. Looking in the mirror, I combed the flames of my hair down onto my shoulders. Wind had made my cheeks eternally pink. Walking had already begun to change my body, sculpting my muscles. I puffed powder between thighs and pulled on a black knit dress, fixed pearls, dabbed red lipstick.

We spent a good half hour fixing a Santa hat on Angel's head. We drank mulled cider, his spiked, and I cooked. He sipped, touched the petal of a white poinsettia on the table, pressed the wax of a red candle, but mainly he watched me at the stove.

"Mnh, mnh," he finally said. "You should wear that dress every day."

"Come on, now," I said in a Southern accent. "This is baby Jesus' birthday."

"We need some mistletoe," he said. "We don't need mistletoe."

When I cleared his plate, the brandy on his mouth tasted like nostalgia to me.

"Do you want your present?" he asked.

I sat on his knee. "Don't pull any naughty-or-nice shit," I warned.

"I got you a good present," he said smugly.

"So give it to me."

I shook the small package. "Mink coat? Cadillac?"

An early edition of *Confessions of an English Opium-Eater.*

"You deserve a first edition, baby, but this cowboy doesn't have the bills."

"You're drunk," I said, laughing.

"Yes. Yes, I am." He stared at the floor with happy resignation. The white Stetson I'd given him tilted at a rakish angle.

"You know what?" I said.

"What," he said.

"I've loved you since the day I met you."

"I know."

The creamy light of dawn let me think I was asleep, and they sounded like dream words. But then he kissed my forehead, and I woke up for real. I rubbed my eyes. His jacket zipped, his good-bye face on.

"Did you hear what I said?" he asked softly.

I shook my head, just to hear it again.

"You know how I was waiting, that it was on the horizon? The greatest thing I'll do, Lee, is be with you."

A couple days later, it snowed enough to coat the streets white. The sun was out, and the world was blinding. On my sidewalk, I passed an old man in an electric-blue tracksuit walking an un-leashed Chihuahua.

"I can't see nothing," he said to no one.

That night I went to a party at a skateboard shop around the corner. A mob crowded the ridges of the half-pipe, which was chicken-wired on all sides. The spectators stood in puddles of melted snow and pulled PBRs from a freestanding bathtub of ice. I watched one kid because I just had a feeling. His hat turned sideways, elbows scarred, and the craziest look, out of all those boys, in his eyes. Moment of silence as his board hung on the lip, and then he dropped in.

Afterward, I had steak and root beer at Diner's counter. Inside, candles painted faces red with light. Outside, blue snow burned in the niches and notches of the towering Williamsburg Bridge.

Later, walking home, I marveled at a shirtless man puking out of the driver's side of a dark gold limousine pulled to the curb. After spitting one last goober, he gave a war cry, threw his legs back into the car, slammed the door, and fishtailed away.

I sketched out the four scenes when I got upstairs. It was the first time I'd really focused in weeks. Before I went to sleep, I stretched four canvases. The pieces would make a diary of the day.

New Year's Eve. It's a promise of a night. Single, married or widowed, in love, loveless or lovelorn, we all leave our apartments and pick through snow in high heels, or descend subway stairs in tuxedos, lured to wherever we're going—whether we know it or not, would deny it or not—by the kiss of a stranger.

Few dinner reservations showed in the blizzard, and those that did were good old downtown natives, eccentric and tolerant.

The staff drank so much champagne they were practically roller-skating from table to table.

Right before midnight, most of us went outside.

Martine always turned ghetto when he was drunk. "Start that countdown, yo. Drop that fucking ball, dog."

"Okay there, Eazy-E," Shannon said, lobbing a snowball.

"I'm-a put a sparkler up your ass," Martine warned.

"Play nice," I said.

"Sorry." Martine dropped his head, truly chagrined.

"Here, baby." I handed him a bouquet of sparklers.

"Tight," he said, started fencing with Ozzie.

We made snow angels in the street. The snow was high, so the angels were deep. Our bodies dropped lavender shadows on the white as we stood, and staggered, out of our silhouettes. The boys all compared wingspan.

Shannon held the phone out the door.

"It's for you," he said. Then, after covering the mouthpiece, he shrugged. "It sounds like Chico."

I reached greedily for the phone, my wet coat heavy as lead on my arms.

"I wanted to tell you first," Chico said.

The street shone like a Rothko: white mounds lit yellow by streetlamps and shadowed in blue. When I finally hung up, I turned to the quiet staff.

"There's a brand new person in the world."

EIGHT

〰〰

The cart before the horse is neither beautiful nor useful. Before we can adorn our houses with beautiful objects the walls must be stripped, and our lives must be stripped, and beautiful housekeeping and beautiful living laid for a foundation: now, a taste for the beautiful is most cultivated out of doors, where there is no house and no housekeeper.

—HENRY DAVID THOREAU, from *Walden*

It's April now. I sit at a gunmetal desk dissecting a jasmine flower fallen from a sprig in the water glass. My fingertips smell like heaven and perfume the handles of my brushes. This room is a riddle with one answer, being too small to arrange any other way. Angel sleeps, moving to stay in the sun like the hand of a sundial. The light turns her coat yellow. Orange sections on a saucer, juice pooling. Springtime comes calling, curls around the window's edges, beckons like a long white glove with no arm inside.

Don't get up, I tell myself. Don't go anywhere.

I'm still in Brooklyn.

It's raining on the Union Square Market. Buckets of lilacs, lilacs for sale. Everyone is selling lilacs, and the lilacs are wet with rain. Riots of white, lavender, and violet disrupt the slick black surface that is the city today. I wouldn't call lilacs lush: the flowerets are prim, and they come too early in the year. But they are generous.

Every spring, I'm reminded that no one has duplicated this scent. Perfumes are built on the oil of lilacs, certainly, and come close to the real thing. But there is nothing scientists can do to replicate the way the essence is released by the plant.

Too many umbrellas in Union Square today. I've just left the restaurant, where I'm still working. I struggle through the crowd with a loaf of bread and a newspaper cone of lilacs.

People duck each other's barbs, almost turn to glance back in dismay, but everyone is dizzy on aromatic rain, so no one gives a damn.

I walk as if following footprints painted on the sidewalk, down the stairs, across the subway platform. Not as fancy as a foxtrot diagram: just the way home.

168 Kent Avenue, #1C.

A ground-floor studio in a warehouse converted to apartments. Barred window looking onto orange mud, river twinkling through fence. Curtain pulled aside. Desk and chair facing out. Jasmine plants on sill.

Wood floor sanded but marked by fossilized burns, stains, digs. New walls. Galley kitchen. Bed, bookcase, stereo, night table. Turquoise horsehide on floor, ballerina on wall.

Vacuum cleaner, mop, bucket, rags, solvents under sink.

Closet. Box of sunglasses, jewelry. Trench coat, Fendi fur, jeans, white sequin skirt, black leather skirt, black tracksuit, black turtleneck, men's V-neck sweater-shirts in black and gray, white T-shirts, white scarf, black underwear and white socks, black flip-flops, black stilettos, black kitten-heel boots, red-and-white Adidas sneakers.

Kitchen. Salt, pepper, herbes de Provence, oil and vinegar, milk, jam, mustard, butter, tea. One bar of soap, one pack of incense, one box of tampons, one stack of toilet paper, and one roll of paper towels. I don't cook much. I make plates of hard-boiled eggs, sausage, cheese, mango. Get the handles of my brushes greasy even though I wipe my fingers on my jeans.

Linen, turpentine, coffee cans, brushes, the alligator briefcase of paints, a palette, an easel.

One vase of lilacs.

◇◇◇◇◇

I picture him on a ladder, in jeans and boots, no shirt. A carpenter apron tied around hips, drill bit between teeth. His broad back swirling with green light and green shadows as wind tosses palm trees.

At night he drinks beers at bars I don't know, and when he leaves the bar, he might get into a friend's pickup, and in silence they'll turn down sandy streets until they get to his house, where the friend stops. When he steps down from the truck cab, he inhales deeply of an island air I don't know. Lying in his bed, he might see a lizard on the wall, and he thinks it's his imagination until it moves. Someone might be lying next to him. When sun comes through the shutter slats, he might miss me. Or he might not.

This is what went wrong.

I'd already packed the apartment on North Seventh Street. My plane ticket was for January 30, in ten days. Wearing bifocals and earmuffs, Art picked me up at the icy, glittering train station. When we walked into their house, the steam of potato and lamb fogged the windows.

Becca wore one of her getups: black tunic, black leggings, and Moroccan slippers. With a Capri in her mouth, bloody Mary on the foyer table, she held a Dustbuster in her hand.

"Oh, my dear!" She shut the tiny vacuum off. "Just last-minute cleaning, you know."

She took a big drag before we hugged, and I heard her exhale over my shoulder. "Let me look at you," she said, holding me away. "Oh," she said, clucking.

We ate the kind of lunch I'd never even make for dinner. Potatoes au gratin, lamb stew. The house was winter dark, and its green walls and Oriental carpets, without being dirty, were oiled by years of life.

Art and Becca were going to rent the other house to Margaret Landry.

"A dear friend of mine," Becca said. "A wonderful, wonderful, *wonderful* writer—and she's bringing a horse—we're making a paddock." Pointing to the window, she drew a vague circle with her hand and ashed on the table accidentally. "Her husband died a few years ago. His liver." She stared at me meaningfully. "Very, very hard on our Margaret. But I tell you, she's stronger than ever. And she looks great, without having had a thing done."

Margaret would use my furniture until I one day had a place to move it all. But I had to deal with the boxes of clothes and papers and jewelry I'd left in the library of the house for two years. Becca wanted to help, insisted it would be fun if we did it together, but I thanked her and declined. Folded my napkin, walked onto the icy field alone. She stood at her open door, smoking, arms crossed against the cold, and waved each time I looked back.

I worked in the library, expecting, as I had each time I'd come out here, the house to reignite with grief like a gas pilot touched by a match. I opened boxes, unfolded dresses, sprayed perfumes, skimmed books. Whatever I'd been afraid to feel, I readied myself to feel.

I clipped on earrings, clusters of blue glass beads that had shimmied and clicked even when she was still. Onto my big wrist, I slid the ivory bangle that used to fall up and down her skinny, freckled arm. I even held to my nose the apricot slip. Lingerie, even if it's washed a hundred times, keeps some trace of the woman. It's the closest thing to a ghost.

The most dangerous objects were in her jewelry box. Strangely enough, things that had belonged to me and become hers were the most radioactive. Previously unbearable, they were what I forced myself to touch that day. My own baby tooth. Grade-school quizzes, in the purple ink of old photocopies, gold starred. A curl of baby hair tied with ribbon.

The worst was an envelope in her bedside table, kept close for when she couldn't sleep. Inside were my letters from boarding school. Most were pages long. As detailed and florid as ancient books hand-copied by monks. On one, I diagram the messy experience of dyeing my roommate's hair pink: there's Lily in the drugstore, then in the room wearing white bib and gloves, me washing the pink from her hair into the sink. A dead deer lies by the roadside, its blood falling up into the sky in teardrops. A rainbow over the dining hall with this caption: *It's Spaghetti Night!!!* Glued to the pages, in between grades and lacrosse scores and art projects, were notes from boys, detention notices, a paper-thin leaf torn from an anthology of poetry, a matchbook from the diner. We missed each other so much when I went away. Nothing could ever be the same. The closest I would come was in mailing these encyclopedias of hopes and fears.

Seeing those letters also reminded me how natural art used to be. How it was not delineated from love. Easy as dipping a sieve in the river and pulling out gold.

Taking what I wanted, and repackaging the rest for Art and Becca's attic, I cried until I had a migraine. But something had changed in my attitude toward her belongings. Now they were souvenirs of love. I would no longer use them as bait. I'd been holding them out like meat to a falcon, hoping to win her back down.

◇◇◇◇◇

Last train out. The snowy suburbs glowed mauve in moonlight.

The first death is like the first crush. Every detail of the beloved, his Big Red breath, her milk-blue earlobe, his pigeon toes, her bobby pins, these details hurt so much they make it hard to breathe. They knock the wind out of you all day long, then all night.

The beloved looms in the mind, obscuring all else. Over and over, his black-and-white-checkered Vans sneaker grinds the cigarette butt, making sparks. Over and over, in a taxi's mirror, she applies rose-scented lipstick to the top lip, then presses lips together. How does anyone else stand to be near him, when everything he does breaks the heart? How can anyone else bear to even think her name, when her name alone, without fail, strikes up a fever of loss? Does no one else suffer? Are they all so blind, shallow, unfeeling?

Then poof. One day it's over. He's still a good kisser, but it's not the same. Her name no longer takes the breath away.

Instantly, we miss that heartbreak, the pain, the dizzy, crazy intoxication of loving too much, loving too hard, loving so the love eclipses the rest of life. And suddenly we feel guilty for letting go, and we feel common for having thought we were singular.

"Ginger," I said as quietly as possible, and one passenger turned. I had to say it again, though, to make sure. "Ginger."

Exhausted, I took a scalding shower when I got home. Huddled in blankets. So dark I couldn't see my hand, and I tried.

No thoughts. More of a physical attempt to register the void of the room, the emptiness of the night. And then I saw her.

Don't know if my eyes were open or closed, but she rose on a geyser of pearls and flames and scarves and doves. My mother came back, radiant as Venus from the shell, in a hot-pink cocktail dress, and real.

These are the pyrotechnics of faith.

I made the phone call the next day. I heard words come out of my mouth and knew how I sounded. Normally, I would have been forceful, insisting he listen and believe. But I had used up all credibility with Kelly Bradley. He'd earned the right to give up.

At first, he tried to change my mind. "Lee, I'll work. It's not expensive to live, and you can paint during the day. You'll have the house to yourself—"

"Baby, it's not that. I don't just need eight hours to be alone. I need to be alone all the time. If I had you, I can't explain it, but I wouldn't do it."

"You sound like you're going into the Army or something."

"I know you think I'm a flake," I said.

He didn't argue. Instead, he was quiet while I explained how I needed to fall apart and be ugly and be useless for everything except living and making money and painting. How I needed to get a toehold on a new life, and had to do it by myself or I'd never be confident it would last.

This is the one mean thing he said: "You've *been* useless."

He apologized, but the apology was bitter since we both knew he was right.

"Maybe we should talk tomorrow after you've slept on this," I suggested carefully.

He snorted, then sighed. "How long is this going to take you, Lee?"

I couldn't lie. "Four months. Three years. I don't really know."

"I'm going to hang up now," he said, already sounding far-away. "And we're not going to talk tomorrow, Lee."

"Kelly," I said, desperate, my mind racing to think of what I meant. "I don't expect you to wait around for me, but, but I will always—"

Click.

I didn't get the chance to explain fully, and at the time, I didn't have the words. But I understand it better now. How my life was top-heavy with love, the foundation of integrity too weak. He would have filled in the empty spaces that I needed to fill myself.

In the past I used men to escape art. But I wanted to disappear, not be anyone's anything. Now I talk like Jules to the canvas. I look in the mirror after hours of work and see a stranger. I smell different in my armpits, between my legs, after a night of painting. My mouth gets rancid.

This body of work in my head requires execution. I won't always live like this, but I have years of paintings to make up before I go forward. An accounting must be done. Before he hung up, I didn't get the chance to point out to Kelly that I was only taking his advice to heart.

So I've assumed half of Kelly's shifts and kept all my manager shifts. In the mornings, I paint. I paint on days off. Every night, even after double shifts, I paint.

This evening I get off the subway. Cherry blossoms confetti the streets. Two girls sell books, gloves, handbags from a tapestry on the sidewalk. The carrottop white girl is dumpy, but the Asian girl traveled here in a time machine from 1969 Paris. Black shards of hair hang from under white leather cap, jeans are tucked into white ankle boots. A morose violet pout sucks on a cigarette.

To get home, I pass Sweetwaters, Level X, Galapagos. Like a dog, I sniff the air. When bar doors open, that heady stink rolls out. I put one foot in front of the other.

Honestly, what I miss most are not the benders, but the coffee with a raspberry danish in the morning, Sancerre with salmon, a cigarette when stuck under an awning in a sudden rainstorm. Not to sound like Nancy Reagan, but any chemical now would open my gate to the others. So when I get home, I take a hot shower, light incense, brew tea, rub Angel, stretch my aching back, close my eyes for five minutes, then sit in front of the easel.

It's usually at this point, looking at a blank canvas, when I think: *Fuck you. I'm not doing this. Holing up like this leads nowhere. This is a farce, another way of hiding. Going out to dance and live and love is braver. I should go out and get my hands dirty. I'm spoiling, like milk left out overnight.* But if I pop the cherry and touch paint to linen, I continue. I've mailed Kelly three small watercolor portraits. They're love letters.

They're also prayers. At the Laundromat the other day, I was reversing pillowcases, and I thought: *Painting doesn't exactly answer my questions, as I'd always thought it would. One painting doesn't suddenly expose the meaning of life. But the process of painting turns doubt inside out. Puts me in a new place, closer to the world. Fortifies my courage. Reminds me that doubt and faith are two sides of the same mystery.*

I've searched the apartment for sketches made over the years. One by one I'm making paintings of these inked vignettes. Kai lying on the couch in chef pants, exhausted from work. The keys, wallet, gram bags, Jolly Ranchers thrown from his pockets onto the floor. Sherry on a moped outside Limelight. A broken glass in the restaurant sink, blood on the tip of Ozzie's finger. Belinda sitting on the subway with a stuffed tiger. A pineapple on Yves's counter. Angel on my bedside table, sniffing a perfume bottle.

It's an overdue diary, an afterword to part of my life.

✕✕✕✕✕

When I was five or six, before the age of reason, my mother confided in me that while I slept, my dolls came alive. This is before the pornography of Ken and Barbie, before the Corvettes and Jacuzzis, before the Sodom and Gomorrah of the pink plastic beach house. The cheeks on these Madame Alexander dolls were apple red. They wore blue felt coats and Mary Janes. Their days were spent changing dresses and pointlessly arguing in haughty voices.

Nighttime was when their little fireplace crackled, a cake baked in the oven, the chandelier glittered. This is when they danced and loved and lost and learned and raced and sang. The welded fingers I pitied during the day certainly opened at night.

I pretended to sleep so I could catch them but always seemed to fall into dreams before they began. In the mornings, my mother pointed out the dolls' exhaustion. I thought they were selfish to exclude me, and I glared at them, but with respect.

Last week I bought a hatbox at a junk shop: flamingo pink, with a forgotten store's name in script on the lid. Now when I finish a new sketch, I lay it in the box. I turn off the light and get into bed and imagine that life on those pages not only continues but maybe even begins. It's the primordial soup of art. When I wake, I find the sum of the pages has added up in the darkness to more than its parts.

Even in the blackest night, my eyes can find a rosy spot under the desk.

Don't look at it. Let it be.

✕✕✕✕✕

I force myself to imagine him at a restaurant, tiki torches reflected in the water, his companions' faces undulating in amber light. The paper place mats show diagrams of knots. The ice of a raw bar glimmers in the background. The strong men have creased necks and brown arms, the stories of waves and shrimp and storms written on their bodies.

Maybe a woman sits next to him, a honey-streaked brunette. Her crow's-feet are deep, her forehead freckled: the summer never ends. Her body shows some effects of fried clams and piña coladas, and is muscular from trimming sails, riding bicycles, planting, weeding. She's beatific, shoulders shiny, and she sits back in her Hawaiian sundress and smiles throughout dinner, one hand on Kelly's blue-jean thigh.

The men stare but catch themselves, clear throats, paw through plates of clamshells and cocktail sauce for napkins they don't need. They concentrate on drinking. If it was anybody but Kelly, they'd be jealous, even wily, but Kelly deserves only good things now. Everyone, after all, knows about the girl up north.

After work today, before I go home, I walk to Chelsea.

Audrey's father's name is Bill. He's come from Oregon on a Greyhound to meet his granddaughter. His chin is plump, with whiskers growing out of tiny dimples, like a strawberry. His clothes smell stale, and every ten minutes he leaves to have a cigarette in the hallway of the building. I get the feeling it's a long wait between smokes.

When he returns, he resumes his place on a kitchen chair, pulled into the bedroom, by the door. He sits as if waiting to be called into an office. Every once in a while, he pats the Winstons in the breast pocket of his flannel. He answers questions, even when he's heard them, with "Mnnh?" followed by "Well, let's see now." His face drags with the disappointments of a rough and ugly life, but his eyes feast on the infant.

Chico drapes a scarf over the lamp because Mabel is asleep, lying the length of Audrey's lap. Mabel clings to her mother's pinkie, dreaming.

I drop by often, bring roast chicken, raisin bread, green-bean salad. I avoid the foods Audrey says are bad for nursing mothers. The assertion I'd made to myself that my friends had forsaken me, and not the other way around, is still privately embarrassing.

I used to treat Audrey like a child. Now I'm grateful to sit here, at the foot of her bed, in a half-lit room and watch her do nothing.

Strolling home, I watch boys skateboard in sleeveless shirts. Their white arms are pink with cold, but it must feel good to ride jacketless. Blustery and delicate winds blow at the same time: one will rip off your hat, the other will riffle your hem. My naked leg feels vulnerable, capable of disintegrating like a sugar cube dropped in water.

An old woman points out to me, as if we're old friends, the crocuses that have survived the late snow of last week.

"Every year they come up earlier," she says, shaking her head at them with reproach, even going so far as to point an agitated finger, as if she didn't like to scold but did so for their own good.

I stop to look at a wedding cake in the window of a Polish bakery. Superimposed on the white tiers: my dark face, wreathed by rust-red hair. The evening air, which has collected from hidden backyards the lilacs, the cherry blossoms, the soil, and the laundry, has driven my heart a bit mad.

Don't get ahead of yourself.

ooooo

My building is so new it smells of paint. I never see anyone. I hear noise from apartments when I walk the hall, and sometimes notice scuffling above me, but I don't know my neighbors. The vestibule is empty now, weak sunlight glinting off the wall of mailboxes that is unscratched, innocent of graffiti. The tiled floor wet from the mop of an unseen janitor.

In my mailbox: a package with Florida postmark.

Inside: the envelopes I'd mailed to him, seals unbroken.

In my apartment, I light incense, brew tea, rub Angel, arch my aching back. I pour tea, but hold the spoonful of honey over the jar, slowly let it drip back. You never know how much it will hurt until it happens.

A returned love letter is written in the most violent language, by your own hand.

"Hey, stranger," Donald says when I finally get him on the phone.

He sounds disappointed to hear from me, but not surprised.

"Hey, sugar," I say, my voice heavy with defeat and regret, although I haven't done anything yet.

After five months, why am I calling? Maybe I've been waiting for a good reason. Why does a girl sleep with her ex-boyfriend? Curiosity. To dare him to win her back. To see if she can tempt him back. To rub his face in what he can't have anymore. Or, sometimes, to celebrate something sweet, and good, and lost.

I knew all along, somewhere deep and dark inside me, that I would do this. I was waiting for the perfect opportunity. A worthy event. I wondered idly if everyone who gets sober plays the same tricks, follows the same AA textbook chapter on pitfalls.

It's Friday night and busy, so Donald sends a runner. Chad and I drink Dewar's and Coke. It tastes like medicine to my newly virgin palate. I sit on my chair, he sits on the bed, as if we're in a dorm room. He's handsome like a model, with flaxen hair and square jaw, but a bit off. His ankles thin as broomsticks, a rash on his hand. He doesn't laugh; he giggles.

He drains his glass, holds out my stuff. I've been building up the strength to cancel. The minute I see the bags and pills, I capitulate.

The goal wasn't up or down, but sideways. The problem is I've lost my touch, and tolerance. Once I get into Black Betty, I can't get out. Alone in a writhing mob. Red lights and hip-hop. A Niagara Falls of sensations. Everything looks greasy: the pearls of that man's eyeballs, the black oil of her leather pants.

I order a drink.

"You already have one," the bartender enunciates.

Crushed against the bar, and I hold on, as the floor tilts like a yacht.

Later, I try to pay. Stare at the money. It's not swimming, it's not that. It jitters, disappears. My eyes can't lock onto the denomination. So I hold bills up like a hand of cards.

"Pick one," I tell the bartender.

Later I'm standing at a door, wet cherry blossoms stuck to my boots.

"Can I help you?" someone asks.

The black kid wears a black knit cap. I can't get my key in the lock.

"What do you want?" I ask fearfully.

He turns away from me, hands on his hips. When he turns back, he has steeled his face. Now he talks slowly, trying not to sound angry. "I asked if I can help you."

With his key, he unlocks the door, invites me to precede him with a sarcastically formal flourish of the wrist. It's the hallway of the building where I used to live. I back away.

"Miss!"

I come back for my bag, which he's picked off the ground. He shakes his head at me, enters the building, slams the door.

I wake up with hot face pressed to cold tile floor. Bright light.

My mother is sitting on my toilet lid, one foot propped on other knee. Cotton stuck between toes. White sleeves of kimono hang. I blink, and she sees I'm awake. Quickly, she replaces wand of red polish.

"Oh, baby," she says, but without anxiety or disdain. "Don't do that again."

I work brunch today. Migraine and nausea, but I pour mimosas for hours because that's my job. I walk home to get air. At the Strand, I look through outdoor shelves without intent to buy. I've been trying to live in this city without disturbing it. If I see a vintage silk blouse blowing on a rack outside a store, I admire and leave it. I treat objects of the city like the butterflies at the museum conservatory that land on your hand but will die if you touch them.

I do, though, have the vague plan to buy something for the guy in the black knit cap, but decide that what he probably wants is never to see my face again. Painting will have to play one more abstract role: apology. Instead, I get a children's book for myself, partly because it's a dollar, and partly for a dose of purity.

At home, I lie on my bed with Angel, orange sunset glazing us both. The fairy book is full of naked children disfigured by long ears or fur. A girl kneels on chubby knees, butterfly wing and petal and stars exploding from her back as if her soul were too big for her body.

Voices trail through the window. A gang tramps across the lot with bamboo poles. One kid's black hair is pinned back like a samurai's. The bleach-blond guy wears a bike chain around his waist. In the twilight, branches snap back after their passage, spewing diamonds of rain.

Tall enough to be eighteen, they betray themselves as younger by their walk, by their laughter. They're not polished. They don't strut. But they do disappear, jumping from rocks to swamp, arms raised like bat wings as they fall. Nothing like getting stoned and going fishing.

And I want to go, to be part of it. Absurd as this is, I yearn after the place where they vanished. But in this life we take turns at being enchanting, then enchanted. First we play in the streets, unaware of the freedom burning in the sun on our hair and the cigarette in our mouth, unconscious of the daydreams we inspire. Then it's our time to sit at a window and watch, and we are moved. Now we get out the brushes and the turpentine.

I make a drawing of Kelly and me into a postcard, hoping he'll look by accident. Hunched over my desk, I'm a portrait of a lost cause. But taking this last chance, licking the stamp and sending the card down the lobby mail slot, I let go of the need to reach him. I resign myself to being alone, which is what I'd demanded in the first place.

Through the vestibule's glass doors that look onto Kent Avenue, I watch a couple carrying a chair, one on each side. The chair must be heavy—their pace is clumsy, slow. The arms of the throne are black ornate wood, the upholstery red silk.

They pause. Set the chair on the roadside in patches of stubborn snow. She sits down on it. He leans. The sky is extremely dark for this hour, and she holds up a palm for rain. He says something, and she laughs. She gets up. They continue their awkward trip.

Don't hate them.

I see Yves all the time. A trench coat in a subway mob, epaulets of rain. A shirt at Cipriani on West Broadway, in a thicket of Europeans and forsythia. At Dean & Deluca, a white-haired man weighing white asparagus as if it were a bundle of dynamite, hesitating the way bachelors do. As I drive by outdoor tables in SoHo, a baby-blue Dunhill box on white tablecloth.

Of course, these are more hypotheses than sightings. *That could have been him.*

Amount by amount, I put money aside. Two hundred and eighty-nine dollars and twenty-three cents one day, ninety-seven dollars and seventy-seven cents another. I would send the money as I make it, but each check will be an insult, so I'd rather do it once. I do understand the inelegance, and I'm sorry for it.

Sometimes I feel that he never existed, that I dreamed up a sugar daddy. Sometimes I think I should be grateful to him, for what he did do when he didn't have to, for what he didn't do when he could have. Sometimes I wake from a wet dream with the abruptness of escaping certain death.

A golden morning in Brooklyn. Lace curtain floats out of a first-story window on Berry Street. The building is mint green. Inside the sill, the red of a child's hair, the white square of music, a black piano that merges with the darkness of the room.

The notes are clear and determined, even when they falter. I could listen to it all day. There's nothing as paralyzing as these keys struck finger by finger, moment by moment. It hypnotizes. While I listen, I'm good for nothing else. This kid is manufacturing innocence.

We meet at the New Museum, wary as bobcats, tails thrashing. Belinda's kept her trademark bangs and bob, but grown heavy in the hips while staying narrow in the chest and lean in the legs. Wearing a tight magenta raincoat, using her zebra-print umbrella as a cane, she attracts attention, more than ever, as though she is a personage.

Inside, we move from painting to painting.

"Oh, I like that a lot."

"Oh, yeah, I like the shimmer there, the heat wave or whatever it is."

"Is that what it is?"

"Well, I don't know. I'm just guessing."

We walk on, fuming with awkwardness, and I regret coming so passionately that I almost decide to go to the ladies' room and disappear.

"Oh, wow. That's crazy. Look at the colors."

"Yeah, it's really vivid. It's almost overwhelming."

Over lunch, we make more silence than conversation. Belinda

sips tea, appraising me, puts the cup down. "You just hate me, don't you."

I stare, agape, truly amazed. "My lord, no."

"You do," she says, smiling faintly.

"It's the other way around," I insist. "You're the one who got it together. I'm the one who fell apart."

"I'm the one who jumped ship," she says, looking into her tea, then at me. "I got all straight and narrow."

"Well, I'm biting your rhymes."

She laughs, runs fingertip on mug's rim. "I'm pregnant again."

My face breaks with pleasure. "That is so wonderful. That's *so* wonderful. Why didn't you tell me?"

She shrugs. She won't talk because her eyes have teared up.

"Oh, sweetheart," I say, reaching for her hand.

"I missed you," she finally says, wiping her eyes.

The box is wrapped in brown paper, postmarked Florida. I take it upstairs, hands shaking.

Inside the cardboard box, an object wrapped in muslin. A page of loose-leaf tucked beside it. The note reads: *Lee, Found this in shed of botanist while renovating. Old guy, cool. He can't remember origin. Maybe Fiji. Plant shallow in deep pot, it might sprout. No promises. K.*

Pull away the fabric, letting the bulb roll in my hand. Big as an ostrich egg, with skin like an avocado. Already, two small white horns have ripped through its leather.

How have I come to talk to you, Ginger? That's a good question. It's a chicken-and-egg situation, I fear. Did I believe you were listening, so I arranged something to say? Or was I moved to speak, knowing you weren't there, then made breathless by awe and joy and relief when you answered?

I see you now, on a mustard-yellow love seat, the velvet worn to a shine, your arm draped over the sofa's back, a sling back hanging casually from your toe. You're so much more relaxed now that you're dead. I like how we dabble, moving straight from your Waldorf salad recipe to the phenomenon of desire. We deal now on the highest level of etiquette: truth.

You shift on the love seat, cross your pale blue legs, almost languorous.

ACKNOWLEDGMENTS

〰〰〰

I'd love to thank my editor, Alexis Washam, and absolutely everyone at Hogarth for this new edition of the book, and many thanks to my agent, Sally Wofford-Girand, too. And here are my thanks as written in the 2004 edition: Jack and Deb, of course. Asya Muchnick. Emily Mead and Alyson Richman, fire-starters. James Swink, Mrs. Richmond, Pat Jones, Marjory Reid, Barry Goldensohn, Steve Stern, Kathryn Davis, Charles Baxter, Eileen Pollack, and Nicholas Delbanco, my teachers. Jake, for help with the Vashon Island Grant. Julien for pellets and inspiration. The Crugers, for the Houston Margarita Madness Grant. Mister Michael Martin and Miss Tobin. Sunny Delight and Duggan's Dew. Dark Crystal, Desmond, Bianca, Kim, Molly and Gabe, Larry, Zoe, Cecilia and Scott, Bruce Mason (figurehead), Gigi, Marisa from Peru, Darling and Gangster, and all the other partners in crime. Love to the angels: Jane, Mary Anne, and Jackie. I know you pulled strings up there.

COPYRIGHT ACKNOWLEDGMENTS

ABOUT THE AUTHOR

⬦⬦⬦⬦

JARDINE LIBAIRE is a graduate of Skidmore College and the University of Michigan MFA program. She is the author of *White Fur* and lives in Austin, Texas.

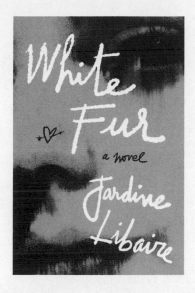

O UTSIDE THEIR MOTEL WINDOW, WYOMING IS LURID WITH SUN-set. A billboard for Winstons simmers on the horizon of highway, as if the cigarettes might ignite in their box.

Standing rain has collected in the sagebrush close to the road, and heat makes a perfume from these puddles: herbal, medicinal, other-worldly.

Inside Room 186 of the Wagon Wheel Inn, Elise will be kneeling on the carpet, which is orange like a tangerine. Her hair is greasy and braided, and a name—tattooed in calligraphy on her neck—is visible. She keeps both hands on the shotgun—the muzzle pressed into Jamey's breast.

He'll be sitting on a chair in the middle of the room, hands on thighs.

"Don't you love me?" he'll ask, quiet and desperate. "Elise. Come on. Don't you love me?"

She bites her lip.

He's not wearing a shirt—just jeans—and his bare feet are splayed. The couple has been in this position for two hours and fourteen minutes.

Fifteen minutes now.

Her muscles are quaking. His should be.

In case the room seems small in this recounting, be sure it's not. It's gigantic, swollen, pounding on a molecular level like a billion hearts, the way a space does when the people in it realize their power. Elise will close her eyes, turn her head, and push the safety off.

CONNECTICUT IS WHERE IT BEGINS.

Elise sits on the couch and listens carefully to this evening's city song of church bells and police sirens. She tilts her long and fine skull in a minor way.

New Haven winter: sour, brittle, gray like ice that forms on milk.

Robbie's place—*and her place too,* Robbie insists—is bare as a squat, with a mattress and thin blankets in each bedroom. The curtains are smoke-soiled. The fridge door is scaled in decals from radio stations and hard-core bands, and stickers peeled off apples. One Lucky Charm lies bloated in the drain.

Taped to her wall, where someone else might hang a crucifix, is a page torn from *Rolling Stone*: Prince in a misty lavender paradise.

Elise moved in three months ago, after Robbie found her snoring in his boyfriend-of-the-night's unlocked Pontiac; she was shivering under a ragged white fur coat.

At first they thought she was a dog.

She squinted at Robbie and his friend, who both stood there with the door open.

"Whoops. This your car?" she'd asked, smiling lopsided, eyes clear, drug-free.

When she stood up out of the backseat, taller than them, a backpack hanging like a pendulum from her hand—then she looked scared. An elegantly sad runaway in generic white sneakers and gold bamboo earrings.

The men had to unclench their fists.

Robbie took her home, and the two became incongruous animals in a fable—a giraffe that helps a honeybee, or a rabbit who saves an elephant, having little adventures from page to page.

The new roommates bonded by cooking macaroni together, dancing in pajamas and socks to Michael Jackson, drinking soda, and watching late-night public access TV. Shit, neither of them has a clue what to do in life except live.

* * *

SHE'S LOOKING OUT her living-room window. Her and Robbie's building is rotted from its eaves down, the floors broken into discount apartment units. Their building has stoic—almost happy—bad health, the way a smile is gleeful if it's missing teeth.

Next door is a white townhouse where two Yale guys live. A chandelier glimmers inside, shining with leftover daylight when everything else is dark. Wealthy families lived there before the neighborhood slipped, and the house is forlorn like a society girl forced to get a job.

These boys happen to be smoking on the porch.

Now Elise is going to do it—before she thinks it over and backs down. It's been driving her crazy.

Now she zips up the knee-length rabbit coat with its vinyl belt, the name *Esther* stitched in violet into the taffeta lining that is threadbare and shimmering. (She traded her can of Pringles for the coat on a Greyhound bus one abnormally warm autumn night, while the factories of Elizabeth, New Jersey, ghosted by in the dark. The black girl was strung out and thought it was a good deal since she wasn't cold at that moment and seemed to revel in the dream she'd never be cold again. *But I already ate some of the chips,* Elise joked in protest, handing over the tube and taking the fur. *No, kid,* the girl murmured, *it's cool.*)

Elise leaves the apartment. Night air snakes into her seams within seconds as she walks down the sidewalk.

Everyone sizes each other up. She waves.

"Hey neighbor," says one guy for the first time since she moved in.

"Hey," she says.

"Where you going?" he asks, obviously intoxicated.

She sniffs and looks away. "Buy some beer."

Her accent is harder than they expected.

"We've got beer."

"What kind?" she says, eyes narrowed.

"The kind," he says, "you don't have to go walking in the cold for."

The three of them amble into the house as if this is an everyday meeting, as if no one is curious about anyone else. Inside, Matt goes to the fridge and pops the caps off three Heinekens.

Elise's heart is a broken machine, crashing and thumping.

"What's your name again?" he asks even though she hasn't said it.

"Elise."

Is she frightening? Is she pretty? The guys blink their eyes as if her body is rippling and morphing and they can't finalize an idea.

She's lanky with round and solid tits. Boys' hips. She's a greyhound, curved to run, aerodynamic, beaten, fast as fuck, born to lose. Her face is stark, outlined by dark cornrows. The features drawn down for velocity. The scalp—ghostly. Her skin and hair verge on oily, but the gray eyes are soft in black-liner confines. A divot in her cheekbone might have come from chicken pox.

"I'm Matt," says the one doing all the talking, his own face appraising, unkind. Nothing happens in his eyes except a vague fizz, like flat root beer.

"And I'm Jamey," says the one with the dimple. He looks like a matinee idol who got drugged—waxy, his eyes heavy with lust but also choirboy chaste.

Jamey.

Somehow he gives the impression of being a hustler, but also being the mark, his self twisted into a Möbius strip of innate glamour and his own exploitation.

"Nice place," she says.

Elise doesn't know what to make of it. A camel-hair coat on a chair. *Interview* magazines and *Wall Street Journals,* cigarette packs and folded twenties and coins and Perrier bottles on the coffee table.

She moves around, in boots and that skanky fur, like an inspector.

"You at Yale?" asks Matt with a straight face, even though they know she's not.

"Nah."

Jamey asks: "Are you from here?"

"From around. You guys from here?"

"We're from New York," Matt says, lighting a smoke, his tone polite considering the absurdity of the question.

"You brothers?" Elise prompts.

"No," says Matt, shaking out the match. "Just look like brothers."

"Grew up together," Jamey adds.

She's watched them since she moved onto the block a few months ago, and could barely tell them apart before tonight. Now it's obvious they're opposites. She's watched as they shaved on the other side of a steamed window, white towel around a waist. They buttoned long coats, getting into their cars where they talked on giant blocks of telephones.

Jamey gets up for another beer.

"Grab me one?" Matt says.

"Me too," Elise adds.

Matt shoots a look to Jamey, who just grins and shrugs, comes back with three bottles.

They sit there, drinking. Elise should go home, but she isn't standing up.

Late at night, Elise has watched them bring home girls in gowns (that drag the dead leaves on the ground) and big tuxedo jackets over their shoulders. Or a girl in a kilt will lean her bicycle against the porch railing and sidle inside on golden afternoons. The boys leave early for classes, hair damp and combed, the world moody with sleep. They wave to the elderly landlord shoveling snow from their walk.

"Well," Matt says in a disingenuous voice. "Bedtime for me."

She's also watched Matt shadow Robbie down the sidewalk to amuse his Ray-Bans-and-Shetland-sweater buddies, without Robbie realizing it (in fact after he'd waved hesitantly to them as he passed), Matt mincing his steps and hanging his wrist, making his face fey and pathetic.

"Guess we'll see you around," Matt says to her forcefully.

"Sure, yeah." Elise lights a Newport King. She stands to blow smoke in his face. "And if you ever get near my friend Robbie again, let alone make fun of him like I seen you do, I'll burn your motherfucking house down."

The blue smoke hangs, waiting, and she looks at him, her eyes half-lidded and suddenly red, deadened. The tiniest smirk touches her mouth.

"I'm sorry, what?" Matt says shrilly.

"You heard me," Elise says, mission accomplished but now having to control her voice from shaking.

"Are you coming into *my* house and telling *me* what to do?" Matt pushes her shoulder, testing the moment.

Elise looks at where he touched her then raises her head to stare at him.

"Okay, Matt. I don't think so," Jamey says, moving between them.

"She's out of here," Matt says to no one.

"You're fucking correct about that," Elise snarls.

Matt points Elise toward the door. "All right, let's move."

"I'll go as fast as I wanna," she says.

She glances back to lock eyes with Jamey, who—with a mystified half smile—is watching her leave.

* * *

ELISE LIES IN her dark bedroom, ashing into a Dr Pepper can next to the mattress.

She's the uncommon baby left in a crib that consoles itself, that can stare for hours at the ceiling. Most people need to sleep once the lights are off, the sex over, and Carson's said good night; something's wrong if they stay awake.

Elise never separates things into day and night, rarely thinks about being a boy or girl, or alive or dead. Without divisions, there's less work to do. She floats, free in a cheap and magic way.

She happily replays what could have happened. She comes from fighters—her mom can drive a stick shift, smoke a cigarette, drink a soda, put on mascara, and deliver a smack to every member of the family without taking her eyes off the highway. Elise could knock that kid's teeth out with a single swing.

She grins into the dark, walks herself around the ring with one arm raised.

But it's the dimpled one, *Jamey*—she didn't know he could exist until tonight; it's like she was watching a jet cross the sky then realized it's a bird. She has to reorient herself.

She didn't leave home last summer with a plan. Twenty years old, she never finished high school, she was half-white and half–Puerto Rican, childless, employed at the time, not lost and not found, not incarcerated, not beautiful and not ugly and not ordinary. She doesn't check any box; her face has Boricua contours and her skin is alabaster.

She left her family and everything she knew the morning after a Sunday barbecue in June. They'd all taken over the grill and picnic tables in the Bridgeport park, the Sally S. Turnbull projects looming in the near distance but far enough away to forget for a few hours.

They sat hunched, swatting at black flies, laughing till they cried. Boom boxes, hot dogs, jean shorts and half shirts, Lay's potato chips, cherry soda, and sunshine that fried their brains and hearts. It was a rapturous last supper. She left the housing unit at dawn, when everyone was sticky with hangover. She walked out the way girls do in campfire stories, heeding a knock on the door that no one else heard, and vanishing.

And she hadn't known why till now. Oh, sweet mercy, now she knows.

* * *

NEW HAVEN IS a skinny, sallow cousin to New York City; it's a town that pretends not to want anything or to need charity. This morning is like most others as the place tries to wake up and get presentable, spilling bums from the alleys, sending parolees to stab litter into a bag, sucking raccoons into drains.

Jamey glides through the cold cityscape, and there are ideas in him, fermenting, the heat of them purring from his mouth.

He walks down the sidewalk behind an old lady leaning into the winter sun. Her plum wool coat is open. Passing, he sees the York Peppermint Pattie of a mole on her jowl.

"Good morning, ma'am," he says, searching her eyes for consciousness.

She doesn't answer.

And he wonders if he meant what he said, if he cares what kind of morning she has. Or if it's just another empty thing he says out loud, a candy wrapper dropped into the street.

In the park, hardy men play speed chess.

The day is warm enough to melt icicles out of trees, making a rain that comes down when it wants, a rain more animal than mineral, a rain with a will, a sentience.

Jamey sees portals—the bubble window of that van, the unlit storefronts, the grate where the gutter ends—his subconscious hunting for patterns since it can't find meaning.

Sometime later, he finds himself drinking coffee from a paper cup, sitting on the steps of a random synagogue. He jumps to his feet, as if he just awoke, surprised to be there, amazed as usual at where he ends up when he hasn't intended to go anywhere.

* * *

JAMEY KNOWS WHAT his advisor meeting will be like, and walks across a courtyard that's shellacked in ice. He tip-taps in suede bucks up the marble stairs, an Ivy League paper doll who holds the door for two rosy-cheeked white girls with books in their arms.

Professor Ford has reached the final stage with Jamey. They started the year amiable, but Ford feels played, disrespected. Jilted.

"Jamey," says Ford, opening his door.

"Hello, sir." Jamey smiles, doomed.

Ford's white hair is carved to the side. "Did you see what Professor Hilden gave you on the paper?"

"I did."

"The class is writing on *Othello* and you hand in a paper on the misunderstood altruism of honeybees."

"I was—"

"I *don't* want to know."

Jamey shuts his mouth.

Ford holds out his palms in an exaggeration of inquiry. "Do you not want to graduate next year then?"

"I do actually want to graduate."

"This has become, by the discrepancies between potential and execution, an insult."

Jamey looks down as he's meant to do while the sun creates a muddy heat from the shelves of clothbound books.

"And I do not care a whit who your father is, nor do I care who your mother is," Ford lies.

Ford is like everyone is and has always been with Jamey: Ford had a crush, he wanted Jamey to like him, he expected the world, and now he hates him because Jamey won't respond.

"I'll do whatever you think is best, Professor Ford," Jamey demurs.

Jamey noticed it early in life. In a group of kids, a parent would speak to Jamey as the other adult in the room. Jamey would look at the floor, but whenever he glanced up, the camp counselor or parent or babysitter was still talking at him.

It even happened with people who had no idea who he was, who never saw his house in *Town & Country,* or read about his parents' divorce in the *National Enquirer,* or relied on his grandfather's predictions as quoted in *Barron's,* who didn't realize they were in the presence of a commodity, a publicly traded stock, a prototype of a child—like Huck Finn or the Little Prince.

If someone were fumbling with their wallet, the drugstore clerk would blush and summon Jamey, next in line: *Let me take care of you while this lady figures her stuff out.* Jamey wasn't impatient; he didn't even notice the line wasn't moving!

When he was little, playing at the Morrisons', Jamey cradled their new pet bunny, and Thomas whined and pulled for a turn—it was *his* bunny after all! Mrs. Morrison warned Thomas to stop, and warned him again, and then she violently grabbed Thomas's little hand off Jamey.

"Let Jamey hold the bunny, Thomas, *goddammit*." Her mouth was bright red and open as she furtively stared at Jamey afterward, and he saw something in her face he would recognize for the rest of his life.

He always thought of these moments later as his "Let Jamey hold the bunny" moments.

People looked to him like one of those Tibetan children picked out as a reincarnated lama. They think he knows the secret to life. They get mad when he doesn't offer it up. What happens, anyway, when the village chooses the wrong kid as their prophet?

* * *

EVERY MORNING MATT waits for Elise to walk by so he can glare at her from the porch, ice hanging from the portico. Sometimes he even vaguely ashes his cigarette in her direction, shivering in his white Oxford.

"You're an asshole," Jamey says when Matt comes inside. "Why are you so threatened by her anyway?"

"I'm not threatened," he says.

"But you are," Jamey corrects him. "She's obviously nothing to you, so why don't you just leave it?"

"Because she *came* into our house."

"We invited her in," Jamey says, stirring hot oatmeal.

"That's because she 'axed' to come in. Doesn't mean she can tell me what to do."

"I don't know. I thought it was hilarious," Jamey says.

"Yeah, it'll be hilarious when our house is on fire," Matt says.

Jamey laughs lusciously, then sighs, and doesn't say anything more. He does this a lot lately.

Matt looks at him like: *What the fuck is going on with you?*

It's strange how much they resemble each other, these two men. But Matt—with his pale skin, dark hair, dark eyes, prominent pointed chin, fine clothes, practiced stances—should be handsome like Jamey. And he's not. There's a sense of moral failing here, the idea that Matt himself is to blame for not being handsome, which somehow makes him uglier.

* * *

ROBBIE IS WHITE and short, and studies airplane mechanics at South Central Community College, and waits tables at Red Lobster. His bowl cut and cornflower-blue eyes are gnome-ish.

With him tonight is a tubby black giant who stoops under the ceiling light.

"What's up, Leesey," Robbie says, chagrined at having yet another guy over.

Sitting cross-legged on the couch, Elise pulls back her sweatshirt hood. "Hey," she says, giving the new guy a once-over.

"Hello there," the guy says in a gracious, Darth Vader–deep voice.

The pair ambles, blushing, into the bedroom, like boys about to play G.I. Joes or Matchbox cars, and Robbie shuts the door softly.

They put on Depeche Mode. Each time a side ends, there's a rustle as someone reaches across the bed to turn the tape over and press Play.

She makes coffee, pages through the newspaper, biting her lip.

Elise grew up listening to her mom have sex in the next room— Denise growling and muttering naughty words—or her cousin giving head in the bed where Elise was sleeping. Hearing other people is arousing and aggravating, the way getting tickled is a mishmash of laughter and the possibility of throwing up.

She puts her hand in her jeans.

* * *

THAT EVENING, Robbie and Elise smoke on the roof, squinting at New Haven's squat and dumpy skyline dusted with stars.

The bedroom window next door lights up.

"Oh shit, that's him," she whispers, awestruck.

"The one with the dimple?"

"I'm getting sorta obsessed," Elise says. "His name is Jamey."

Robbie smiles uncomfortably. "They're rich kids. You know that, right?"

"Yeah, I know."

Robbie flicks ash into the abyss between houses, and the coal is fired up by its twirling descent for a second or two. "You like him though?"

Now Elise is shy. "He seems different."

They toss cigarettes over the ledge, pull coats tight, and take the steps down into the building.

"I guess you never know, honey," Robbie says over his shoulder. "Right?"

"Right?" she answers.

Elise trusts Robbie on a gut level. She gets being bisexual, and thinks everyone is attracted to anyone, but gay boys have it rough, they learn fast and cruel. This one kid who worked at a check-cashing place in her old neighborhood was famous for being queer. He was all buttoned up, saving money, determined to get out of that town, always wearing neckties and cardigans, polite in the Plexiglas booth, but he wouldn't hide his wrists or pursed mouth. She walked in there once with her Burger King check, and he was swollen, one eye bandaged, one ear burned. Necktie in place—green polyester with diagonal maroon stripes. She was fascinated by him—nearly destroyed for love, over and over, and refusing to lie.

She survived years of school fights herself, fights that came from real and imagined sexual and social conflicts. She knew what it was like to be forced to take the squatting posture against another girl in the parking lot, hair in her face and mouth, a tribe watching, a random extra girl coming into the fight once in a while to kick or punch, the creepy silence broken with huffing and a whimper. No matter how bad Elise got hurt, she never regretted standing up for herself. She was glad when that stage—fighting every week—was over. Although you have to be on guard forever.